THE TROUBLE WITH MUMMIES

F.R. HITCHCOCK

D0815674

HOT
KEY
BOOKS

First published in Great Britain in 2013 by Hot Key Books
Northburgh House, 10 Northburgh Street, London EC1V 0AT

A CIP catalogue record for this book is
available from the British Library.

ISBN: 978-1-4714-0046-9

1

Typeset by Palimpsest Book Production Limited, Falkirk, Stirlingshire
This book is set in 11.5pt JoannaMT

Printed and bound by Clays Ltd, St Ives Plc

Hot Key Books supports the Forest Stewardship Council (FSC), the
leading international forest certification organisation, and is committed
to printing only on Greenpeace-approved FSC-certified paper.

www.hotkeybooks.com

For Mummies and Daddies,

young and old,

ancient and modern

Chapter 1

Probably the first really noticeable thing was Mum coming back from the hairdresser's on Friday afternoon, wearing a small black beard.

I sat at the kitchen table, staring.

'What?'

'Mum? You've got something...'

'Yes, Sam, dear?'

'Mum – you've got a beard.'

Mum stood in front of the tiny mirror stuck by the back door.

'Yes, dear – don't you like it?'

It's Saturday, and Mum's beard hasn't gone away.

She's up in the bathroom right now, wrapping it in tinfoil.

'Sam,' says Dad. He pulls on his jacket. 'Would you like to come into work with me?'

I nearly choke on my cereal. He knows I can't stand his work. Dad runs the City Museum. The really boring, really big City Museum stuffed full of stuffed things in dusty boxes; beyond your wildest dreams of boring. It's so dull that you have to leave your brain behind at the door to stand it for more than a minute. Dad manages to make it even more boring by giving the same tour every time we go round. If I have to listen to it again, I think I might actually be sick.

'Um…' I stare at my spoon and hope that this might blow over on its own.

'I know you hate the museum, but…' Dad pours himself a cup of coffee, and slurps half of it down, '…I thought that just this once, you might like a wander round before we reopen to the public on Monday? It's changed in there, really. We've updated it. I'd love to see what you think.'

I'm still staring at my spoon.

'I'm driving; you won't even have to walk,' says Dad.

I shake my head. 'No thanks.'

'Perhaps you could bring Ursula?' Dad checks his tie in the mirror. 'We could pick her up on the way. She could bring her camera – go behind the scenes, while it's all fresh and new? Record it for posterity.'

'No thanks, really. Dad? Have you noticed that Mum's got a beard?'

'Yes, good, isn't it?' He glugs down the rest of his coffee. 'The builders are finally moving out of the museum – they've redone everything; they've even installed air conditioning. It's all terribly exciting – it feels like a rebirth.'

I stare at him. Sometimes I worry about someone who can get this excited about dead people and air conditioning.

'The museum's just like a new baby – it needs visiting, welcoming. It needs young friends. Friends like you and Ursula.'

Dad really hates to give up.

'What? When?' says Ursula, camera bags dangling from her wrists.

'Now, in a minute – Dad's outside in the car, he'll take us round, it won't take long – I agreed just to keep him happy.'

Ursula raises an eyebrow. 'Honestly, Sam – don't you know how to say "no"?'

We walk into the newly cleaned-up hallway of the museum. It's all very shiny and light. It seems bigger, taller. It used to be crammed with stuffed birds in cases, stuck onto broken twigs and labelled with curly brown scraps of typing. Now there's a huge TV showing floaty skeletons and cave paintings.

'Where's the dodo gone?' asks Ursula.

'Sorry – it went to auction – same with the cassowaries and the hummingbirds. We thought we'd get modern, so we've got an interactive monitor coming with films of birds in their natural habitat. Good, eh?' Dad presses a button and a pair of glass doors glides open. 'This way,' he says, sweeping us through.

'Wow!' says Ursula, snapping away with her camera. 'Impressive.'

It is impressive, for a museum. There's a bank of glass cases, glittering with cleaned-up Egyptian relics. It used to be a single dusty case that looked more like a jumble sale than an exhibit, crammed full of sarcophagi and jars. The doors to some of the cases are open, and serious-looking people in white gloves are rearranging the neat white labels. I wouldn't go so far as to call it a new baby, but they've certainly spent some money.

I'm almost tempted to read one of the labels, but I discover the floor's been polished and that I can skid all the way from one end of the room to the other. 'Wheeeeeeeeeeee,' I cry.

'Sam!' Dad looks pained.

'Sorry,' I say, trying to look serious.

'We've cleaned everything,' says Dad. 'Recatalogued. Taken out some of the questionable items.'

'Like what?' asks Ursula, filming one of the open cases.

'Odd things. All impossible to authenticate and not really of archaeological interest.'

'What did you do with those?' asks Ursula, her camera trained on his face.

But Dad's ahead of us now, running his fingers over the gold painting on a sarcophagus. For a moment, in the reflected light, he looks a little mad.

'Are you meant to do that, Dad?' I ask. I've never been allowed to touch anything – that's partly why I hate the place so much.

'What?' Dad looks surprised and steps back. 'Sorry, I don't know what came over me – no, I'm absolutely not.'

I look at the sarcophagus he was stroking. It's got a beard too, just like Mum's. I look at the label; it's not a man, it's a woman. A pharoah-ess, presumably. How curious. Bearded Egyptian women; something I've never noticed before. Perhaps it's a new fashion?

'C'mon, Sam.' Dad whisks us through the rest of the downstairs. Ursula films it all, but then she films almost everything. We wind up at the refurbished gift shop.

5

It's the same old tat, but the shelves are shinier. A kit of a catapult that will never work properly; a bent arrow and bow; a plastic Viking sword; a pencil sharpener in the shape of a funerary jar. I pick through the guns in case there's one I haven't got.

'So – did you enjoy that? Record it all?' Dad asks Ursula. He's playing with a paper sarcophagus mask; he holds it up over his face. 'We could do the Americas now, upstairs. It's been revamped.'

Ursula fiddles with her camera case.

'Actually, could you take us home?' I ask. 'I was thinking of taking my Derf guns onto the common.'

'Yeah, I could film you,' says Ursula.

'I can't tempt you with the bloodthirsty Aztecs then?'

'Um, not really, thanks, Dad. I'm kind of museumed out.'

Dad opens his mouth to plead with Ursula, but she interrupts him. 'Yes, Mr Lloyd, I think we've had enough of history. For today.'

Chapter 2

On Sunday night, after we've eaten a strange supper mainly made of cucumber, Finn sits on the floor filling up on chocolate, Dad watches Marcus shooting aliens on the games box, and I watch Mum.

She's been painting on the walls with black poster paint.

She takes the brush and marks out a long rectangle that goes from top to bottom of the wall, running right over the flowery wallpaper that she made Dad put up last summer. She places a small black bird at the top, and an eye beneath it.

'Dad!' I say, pointing at Mum.

'Yes,' he says mildly, reaching for a building supplies catalogue. 'A cartouche.'

'But why's Mum painting on the walls?'

'I don't know,' he says, examining a page of sand. 'I expect she feels like it.'

Marcus, my older brother, glances up from the carnage on the screen. He raises an eyebrow, but looks back just in time to shoot an approaching space squid.

Mum fills the rest of the rectangle with symbols: birds, fish, snakes and things I can't recognise. Mum's not a very good painter.

'Hieroglyphics?' I say.

'Mm, very good, Sam,' says Mum, marking out another rectangle on the wall. I look around. There's not a scrap of flowery wallpaper showing now, nothing but eyes and birds.

I stare at Marcus's screen aliens. Just for now, they seem more normal.

The next morning on my way to school I worry about Mum. Actually, I've been worrying about Mum all night. Perhaps I should call the doctor? But then, Dad would have done that. Wouldn't he? If he was worried? I'm worried that he's not worried. I look at everything in a new light as I walk through the estate. I imagine myself as a motherless child, wild, unwashed, having to make my own packed lunches. I pass a woman who looks like

Mum's hairdresser painting a brown deer thing on her front wall; I'd be hanging round at houses like hers, hoping for food, begging a Sunday roast. I'd become one of those kids at school who never have the right PE kit, all because my mum's gone off to be a fairground attraction as a bearded lady.

I decide that when I get home from school, I'll tackle her, or Dad; whoever seems more likely to listen. I'm just making up my mind which one I'll go for when I see Ursula. 'Ursula,' I whisper. 'My mum's got a beard.'

'So?' she says. 'The headmistress's got a beard, or at least hairs on her chin – bearded ladies are all the rage around here.'

We dodge through the playground, ignoring the twins who try to trip us up, and Ricky Smetling, who's galloping around on an invisible horse.

'It's not a two hairs kind of beard, it's an Egyptian beard,' I say. 'You have to see it to know what I mean.' I run along behind Ursula, who seems to be in a hurry this morning. Actually, she's generally in a hurry. 'And Mum's painted the house with Egyptian symbols, big black birds all over the walls. Dad doesn't seem a bit fussed, only I'm worried about her – apart from anything else, she's only eating cucumber.'

The twins' older brother, Henry Waters, lumbers towards us. He's brick-shaped, and brick-coloured. His hair stands up on his head like a scrubbing brush, and he's always got bits of food on his sweatshirt. He's a monster to look at but he's got the heart of a puppy. He's really soft, and kind, and always does the right thing. If you were ever looking for someone to play 'Brick Boy, Superhero', Henry would be the one, but he can only play a brick. He completely ruined Ursula's last film, *Revenge of the Zombie Tortoises*; he played the policeman that got licked to death in the first scene. Ursula can't stand him.

'Hi, Sam. Hi, Ursula – cucumber? Sounds good, are you making a film about giant vegetables? Having any ideas? Need any ideas?' He moves his weight from side to side as if he's dodging punches. 'Need any actors?'

'Henry,' says Ursula. 'What do you want? This is a private conversation, go away.'

Henry stops; for a moment his face wavers, like he's about to cry. 'Just asking,' he mumbles, wandering off to the side, like someone pulled the plug.

Sometimes, I really don't like Ursula.

Chapter 3

In class, Miss Primrose, our form teacher, sits on her desk, nursing a huge mug of coffee.

Miss Primrose is usually lovely. She's usually fluffy-kittens-in-a-basket lovely. She gives off a faint smell of clean things, and wears peachy-pink nail varnish.

'Morning, class. Now, this week, we were going to study biodiversity, but d'you know, I think we'll make a start on cultural diversity instead.' There's something about the way she says this that puts me on alert. A vacancy in her eye that reminds me of the way Mum's behaving. Perhaps her eyes aren't looking *at* us so much as *over* us.

Maria Snetter, the vicar's daughter, sticks up her hand. 'Does that mean studying the church, miss?'

'Possibly,' says Miss Primrose, drawing a long snake

around the edge of the board. 'But I was thinking of a culture much further away from home.'

'India?' asks Harish.

'India?' Miss Primrose stares dreamily out of the window. 'It might be very interesting – but I'm feeling more South American.' She wanders over to the window and picks up a feather from the making tray. 'Yes, Mexico in particular.'

I hear a tiny high whine, and I realise that it's Ursula's camera. She must be filming from under her book.

Miss Primrose wanders back to the whiteboard and writes: '*Tenochtitlan*.' She turns to face us. 'The great city of the Aztec empire. Now, does anyone know anything about them?'

Maria Snetter sticks up her hand. 'They worshipped the sun?'

'They did,' says Miss Primrose. 'Anyone know anything else?'

'They made floating gardens, and they had a feathered snake god called Quetz-something,' says Rani Race.

'Very good.'

'Didn't they drink blood?' asks Ursula.

'They probably didn't drink blood, but they were a highly ritualised society.'

'What's "highly ritualised", miss?' asks Will Katanga.

'Killing babies!' yells Ricky, leaping from his desk and charging round stabbing everyone with a pencil case.

Miss Primrose ignores him, slicing the top from an old pillow with a craft knife. Thousands of feathers burst out of the cut and drift across the classroom, clustering under the desks, but Miss Primrose doesn't seem to mind. 'Now, I'd like some of you to find out some more about the Aztecs; what they ate, how they lived.' She pulls a large black rubber thing and a tub of PVA glue from behind the desk. 'Ursula, Sam and Henry, you can go to the library and look up the Aztecs, and the rest of you can help me stick feathers on this wetsuit to make a priest's costume.'

Henry lags behind on the way to the library, and I do my best to lag behind with him.

'C'mon, Sam,' says Ursula. 'Hurry up.' She swings into the library, letting the door slam behind her.

I wish it wasn't the three of us together. It's difficult being with Henry *and* Ursula: if I side too much with Henry then Ursula gets prickly; the other way, and Henry looks like I've slapped him.

And I'm stuck in the middle.

I push open the library door. Ursula's slumped over the

desk, drawing vampires on the back of her hand. Henry and I stand in awkward silence next to the history section. He pulls out a book about South America. I find another, and open it on the desk, well clear of Ursula's sprawling arms. Henry flicks through the books. 'Here they are.' He points at some pictures. 'Shall I photocopy these bits?'

Ursula waves her arm at him as if he could photocopy the whole library if he wanted. 'I'm bored,' she announces. 'This is the most boring place in the whole world, and the library's probably the most boring part of it.'

'Well, my house isn't,' I say. 'Boring, that is. And I don't think Miss Primrose is boring today – in fact, I think she's gone weird, like Mum.' I hold the photocopier lid open for Henry.

'She's just like normal – Miss Primrose is normal, she's the essence of normal. Nothing more normal and ordinary than Miss Primrose could possibly exist,' spits Ursula, pushing the photocopies to one side. 'Too much time spent here makes you imagine things, Sam. I bet Mary Shelley was having a really boring time when she wrote *Frankenstein*.'

I watch the machine spit sheets of copied paper into the tray and think back to Miss Primrose in the classroom. The way she let those feathers spread all over the place.

Adults never do anything like that – they're always rushing around with dustpans. 'I think she's gone mad, like my mum.'

'Hey,' says Henry. 'Look at this.' He points to a pile of carefully arranged books, two candles balanced on top and a green lump of plasticine in the middle. The candles are lit.

'What is that?' I say. 'And why haven't the smoke detectors gone off?'

'Because,' says Henry, pointing at the empty battery compartment of the overhead smoke detector.

'It looks,' says Ursula, 'like a shrine.' She focuses her camera on one of the candles.

'To what?' asks Henry, picking up the plasticine lump and pulling it into the shape of a snail.

'Plasticine, of course, stupid,' says Ursula.

'Now you've got to admit something's going on,' I say, backing away from the shrine.

Ursula slumps back at the table, and looks through the pictures on her camera. 'Sam – I really think you're getting in a twit about this. Miss Primrose is reconstructing something because we're studying it. If you remember, we built a grass hut and tried eating custard apples when we did Captain Cook, and I expect another class is studying...

shrines.' She glares up at me as if I'm wasting her time.

'To be fair to Sam,' says Henry, after a considered pause, 'that business with the feathers is unusual; I've never seen her behave like that. I've never seen any adult behave like that.'

'And my mum, with the beard?' I ask.

'Oh, honestly,' says Ursula.

'Beard?' asks Henry, sitting down too close to me. 'Your mum's got a beard?'

I walk home with Henry. He's all bouncy and keen, but I feel faintly sick, partly because I'm sure something's going on and the only person who believes me is Henry, and partly because I'm exhausted by trying to keep the peace between him and Ursula.

I'm quite cross with Ursula; not that I'd ever tell her.

We walk past the new museum cafe. It's already open and a divine smell of chocolate and coffee fills the air outside. We stop for a second to look into the window display. Alongside the bags of coffee beans, and 'raw' chocolate, wonderful cakes rise. Huge curls of chocolate fall delicately over scale cake models of Stonehenge and the Acropolis.

'Wow,' says Henry. 'Makes you hungry.' He grabs a wodge

of biscuits from his backpack and crams them into his mouth.

'Yes – it does,' I say. 'Henry?'

'Yes?'

'Do you think I'm worrying about nothing?'

'What are you worrying about?' We walk on out of the town square.

'All the odd stuff. I mean, Miss Primrose isn't as odd as Mum, but she's definitely heading that way; it's as if they've caught some bug. And there's that shrine in the library.'

Two members of the rugby club march across the road and onto the pavement in front of us. They're chanting something. 'Sinister, dexter, sinister, dexter.' One of them trips on the kerb. 'Dexter, sinis…dex…dex…sinister, dexter. Consiste!' they shout together. They pause, stamping their feet in time outside the rugby club shed. The smaller one pulls open the door and they march in, greeted by a huge chant of 'AVE!'

We watch them disappear inside. 'I'm sure that's Latin,' I say. 'I'm sure Dad said something about sinister being left, and dexter being right.'

'Fancy the rugby club being able to speak Latin. Perhaps they've always spoken Latin. Perhaps rugby's played in Latin,' says Henry, stuffing the end of his lunch sandwiches into his mouth; the crumbs tumble down over his sweat-shirt.

'I don't think so,' I say. 'Anyway, Mr Dent's part of the rugby club – he has enough trouble speaking English, let alone Latin.' Mr Dent's our PE teacher.

We walk on, but Henry turns to look back at the rugby club shed. 'Now you mention it,' says Henry, 'that Latin business is definitely strange.'

I leave Henry near his house and take a short cut over the common.

In the distance a digger slices a long line of turf from the cricket pitch. I wonder if I should tell someone, because I don't think it's supposed to be there; it doesn't look like a good thing to do before the cricket season.

Perhaps the rugby club is sabotaging the cricket club.

I think about the marching rugby players; they seemed quite cheerful, but Henry was right, it was definitely strange. And worrying.

Romans? Egyptians? Aztecs? And those cakes?

No – it can't be, the historical thing must just be a coincidence.

Surely.

Dad pulls up beside me. 'Lift?' he asks.

I climb in. He's listening to twangy music on the car stereo. 'What's this?'

'Ancient music, from the Ptolomeic period. I found the cassette in the museum. Rather nice, isn't it?'

Nice? I'd rather eat porridge.

'Dad, there are lots of…odd things happening around the place. I mean, is "Aa-ve" a Roman thing?'

'Yes – it means "greetings", but you can't trust those Romans,' says Dad. 'Always up to new tricks. Violent lot. Now us Egyptians…'

Us?

Egyptians?

Chapter 4

Something's happened to the back garden.

It isn't there any more.

Mum's vegetable patch, the lawn, the pond: all gone, and instead, there's a square of blocks, squidged together with cementy glue. It looks like a giant two-year-old's been let loose with a Battenberg cake and butter icing, except it's big, really big. It takes up the whole space.

My heart practically stops.

'Dad?' I say. 'What's that?'

He takes a chair out of the boot of the car. A really old, Ancient Egyptian chair, painted in golds and turquoises. I last saw it in the museum on Saturday.

'Something your mother's building.'

I follow him through the front door.

The hall is red. Blood red. A border of wobbly fish and

birds now lies just above the skirting board, and my great-grandmother's portrait has been replaced by a badly painted snake. Underfoot, the carpets have gone; instead someone's emptied damp sand onto the chipboard and I don't really want to go any further, but I can't stay in the hall forever. I push open the door to the sitting room.

Marcus is sitting there, shooting aliens on the television screen and shouting at his friends online. He's still in his school uniform.

'Marcus?' I ask.

Pwew

Pwew

'Yeah,' says Marcus, destroying a virtual wall.

'Have you looked outside?'

Marcus shrugs while his avatar climbs into a virtual quad bike and crashes into a virtual tree. 'Yeah, but no one's told me to tidy my room for a week, so it can only be good.'

I go through to the kitchen. Mum's wearing her best cocktail dress and mixing cement on the kitchen floor.

'Hello, Sam, love,' she says, smiling. 'How's school?'

'Fine, Mum,' I say, helping myself to a biscuit. 'Mum – are you OK?'

Mum looks up at me, smiling. 'Never better. Having the time of my life,' she says. 'Why?'

'Because…' I wave my arms over the mess. 'Because of all this.'

Mum shrugs. 'I'm fine, but thanks for asking.'

I go back into the sitting room. Something moves in the corner. It's Finn and the cat. Or at least, I think it's the cat.

Finn's kneeling on a heap of sheets, torn into strips, and something's wriggling in the middle.

'Meeerreoooow.' It is the cat.

'Shh, puss cat,' says Finn, grabbing a length of sheet. 'Stay still.'

'Finn, what are you doing?' I ask.

'Keeping the cat warm.'

'I think Smudge is fine how she is,' I say, pulling away a strip of cloth.

'No – she needs wrapping, like the teddies.'

'The teddies? I ask. 'What have you done to them?'

'They're ready to cross the River Nile,' says Finn happily.

'Where are they, Finn?'

'Over there.' He points towards the study door.

Feeling sick, I tiptoe past the flailing cat and push open the door to the study. Lined up inside, arranged across the printer and the keyboard, are a series of shapes. They're wrapped in an assortment of materials from loo paper to socks. Mostly there's nothing sticking out, but I recognise Finn's favourite teddy, because his two blue plastic eyes shine out from behind the bandages.

My heart stops again.

'Weird, aren't they,' says Marcus, shooting another alien. 'Creeeeeeepy, ooooooooooohhh.'

'I think they're lovely,' says Mum. 'Well done, Finn. What a clever boy.'

Chapter 5

Mum serves cucumbers again for supper. Marcus says he's not hungry and goes off to shoot more aliens on his smartphone and eat some of his secret supply of Jaffa cakes. I sit at the table, watching the rest of my family and wondering what it's like to be an orphan. Very like this, I imagine. I seem to have lost my family and inherited someone else's. I quickly run through the options of people I could go to for help. Mum? No. Dad? No. The doctor? I'm too scared of him ever since he told me off for sticking a pencil rubber up my nose. Marcus? Worse than useless. Miss Primrose? Absolutely not.

So all I've got is Ursula and Henry, and Ursula doesn't believe me and I'm not at all sure how much use Henry'll be, especially as we don't actually know what's wrong with them, except for an extreme love of fancy dress. I certainly wouldn't know how to cure them.

Mum's got thick make-up all round her eyes, and her hair's now short and black. It doesn't look like it's dyed, it looks more like the string mop that's been mouldering outside the back door for months dipped in poster paint, and she's still got the beard.

'Dad,' I say, stroking the back of the Egyptian throne from the museum. 'Are you supposed to be using the things from the museum – aren't they really too precious for us to have in the house?' I ask it as casually as I can.

'S'all right,' he says, tightening the towel around his waist. He's wearing a vest, and shoes and socks, so just at the moment he looks like an ordinary bloke who sat in something by accident and had to change his trousers, but I don't think that's why he's wearing the towel. 'No one minds.'

'But what are you doing?' I ask. 'What's all this for?'

Mum looks at me, and for a second her eyes go normal, then she goes back to being the extra-smiley thing she seems to have become. Marcus is right, no one's been told off for a week, even Finn, who's been stuffing his face with chocolate all the time. I should have noticed.

'Home-made ice cream? Sam?' she says, whisking a box out of the freezer. 'Or home-made sweets?'

She puts a saucer of brown blobs on the table. I can see they've got nuts sticking out of them and they might be made of dates. 'They're sweets?'

'Original Egyptian recipe, authentic ingredients,' says Mum.

Dad picks one up and pops it in his mouth. 'Delicious, love. Cinnamon?'

'Yes – and cardamom.' She holds the plate towards me, Finn grabs two and I take one. 'The ice cream's made with real chocolate, from the museum cafe.'

They all watch me while I eat the sweets, as if I might explode. But they're actually quite pleasant. So I have another, and another, and then try mixing them with some of the ice cream that Mum plonks in bowls, and then quite quickly have some more ice cream. Gradually I stop feeling so worried. The ice cream's really nice, the sweets are fine, Mum seems happy, Dad seems happy, Finn seems happy.

So, with the help of some more ice cream, I'm happy too.

* * *

I'm running. Racing through the jungle, through big heavy wet trees and things that hiss in the undergrowth. My legs are ridiculously heavy, so that my top half seems to be miles ahead of my bottom half.

In the distance I can hear drums, heavy slow drums.

Tendrils lash my face; hands reach out of the mud and grab at my wellingtons.

I run faster, skimming over the ground, and suddenly my legs take huge strides, racing ahead so that the plants on either side become a green blur. Faster, faster, so fast I can't even see the ground, and I burst through the trees to the edge of a lake.

I stop, not needing to breathe, not even remotely out of breath.

Stretching out before me is a causeway. Although in the back of my mind I know it's a bad idea, I step onto it and walk between little vegetable plots, growing corn on the cob, to a city. The walk seems a long way, so I stretch my arms out and fly some of it before gently landing in a crowd. They gasp and rush towards me, grabbing at me, lifting me over their heads and towards a tall stepped pyramid. They drop me at the foot, and a man with several stuffed parrots on his head and a feather-covered wetsuit comes towards me, his bony hands closing around my wrist.

He might be the school caretaker. I pull back, but I slip, and looking down I see the steps of the pyramid are slick with blood. I try again, but the crowd pushes me up the steps, and the parrot man pulls until I reach the top.

The crowd cheers and points at the parrot man.

He's got a knife, a huge silver tinfoil knife, and he raises it high above my chest...

Brrrinnnggggg.

My bedroom walls reflect the morning light. No blood, no pyramid, no parrot man.

Phew.

Chapter 6

On my way to school, I have to pass the police station. I walk about fifty steps further on, before plucking up courage and retracing my steps. I'm not overly fond of the police. They're mostly big and scary, belong to the rugby club and make jokes that I don't understand – but I think the time has come to face my fears. After all, what's scarier – your family going mad? Or a big bloke from the rugby club making jokes at your expense?

'Hello there. How can we help?' says the huge man leering over the counter.

I swallow. This sounds so stupid. 'My mum's gone mad, she's painted cartouches all over the sitting room.'

'Car-whats?' says the policeman.

I swallow again. 'Cartouches – Egyptian symbol things, hieroglyphics?'

The policeman glugs something from a mug and nods as if he's understood.

'And my dad, he doesn't seem to think there's anything wrong. In fact he's dug a well where the patio ought to be and they've got rid of the carpets and covered the floor in sand. And my teacher, Miss Primrose, has gone weird, too. She's covering a wetsuit in feathers, and someone's built a shrine in the school library.'

'Not a criminal offence as far as I'm aware.'

'No, but it's odd – someone needs to investigate. I think something's happened to them.'

'Oh!' says the policeman. 'And what do you want me to do about it?'

I shrug. 'Stop them?'

The policeman leans on the counter and looks up at the clock. 'Tell you what – I'll be round later on. I'll come to your school first.'

'Shakespeare Primary,' I say. 'When will you come?'

'S'afternoon,' he says, leaning back and scratching his back against the wall, like a cow. 'At the end of my shift.' He comes to open the front door to let me out. 'Don't worry, lad, we'll sort it out.'

* * *

'The sun god,' says Miss Primrose, 'will require a huge celebration, to make him reappear after the eclipse.'

Miss Primrose is wearing the wetsuit; it's completely covered in feathers. She's building a stepped pyramid out of chairs. When she's not stacking up the chairs, she picks up a little tippy barrel thing that makes dying cow noises and rocks it.

'*Mooooaaaaaahic.*'

'*Mooooaaaaaaa.*'

I don't think it's particularly Aztec. More Christmas Stocking.

'*Mooooooooooaaaaaaahic.*'

On her head is a bike helmet studded with bottle tops. Leaning against her desk, a broom handle decorated with feathers, drinks cans and supermarket carrier bags. She's like the man with the knife in my dream, but then again, she's not, because she's Miss Primrose, and Miss Primrose is a basket of kittens.

Because Miss Primrose has stolen the chairs, we're all sitting cross-legged on the floor, except for Ursula, who's sitting on a pile of books under a desk.

'When's the eclipse, miss?' asks Ricky, feeding feathers to Cedric the class hamster.

'Next week. It's only a little one, but we need to look

33

at our calendar.' Miss Primrose pulls out two bin lids painted with symbols and revolves them one against the other. 'The thing is, children, the universe is very delicately balanced. The gods are always competing for power, and they could upset the universe at any point.'

Will looks ready to cry.

'We have to make sure we appease each god at the right time; this calendar helps us get this right. One of the most important gods in Aztec culture is the sun.'

Looking at the bin lids, I can't see how they can help anything. Ursula's camera whirrs under the desk. I look across and she smiles.

'This here,' Miss Primrose points to a green squiggle on one of the bin lids, 'is a crocodile, and if I revolve it here, it points to...'

For a moment, staring at the symbols, I'm drawn back into my dream, and then I remember that Miss Primrose is helping us study the Aztecs, so of course she's dressed up. She's just pointing to pictures on bin lids, she's not a high priest on a temple top.

Henry Waters sticks up his hand. 'Miss, what about the sun? You were saying about the sun?'

'Oh yes, Henry, the sun is terribly important. Their original creation myth, the myth of the fifth age, which is the age we're living in now, is all about the sun and keeping it moving in the heavens, so we need to bear that in mind when preparing our celebration.'

'What's the myth, Miss?' asks Ricky. 'Is it bloodthirsty?'

'No – it's lovely, maybe a little...hot,' says Miss Primrose. 'You see, one of the gods was chosen to be the sun; his name was Tecciztecatl.' Miss Primrose tells the story as if it was *The Three Bears*. 'He was rich and powerful, but to become the sun, he had to throw himself into a pit of raging fire that all the gods had built. Another god, a far less proud one, covered in sores, was to become the moon. He was called Nanauatl. The two gods stood looking into the flames, and Tecciztecatl lost his nerve.' Miss Primrose laughs at this, as if it was a great joke. 'Instead, without making any fuss, Nanauatl threw himself in – wasn't that nice of him?' She looks round at us. Most of the class look blank, some look panicky, and Will starts to cry in earnest. 'So, embarrassed, Tecciztecatl jumped in too, and after they'd been consumed by the fire, two suns appeared in the heavens. The other gods were so shocked by Tecciztecatl's cowardice, one of them threw a rabbit into the sky, clouding the second sun and creating the moon, which is why the moon looks like a rabbit.'

I look round. It's obvious that no one's ever thought of

the moon as a rabbit. Will's rubbing his tears onto his sleeve. I look back at Miss Primrose. She's drawing a big fire on the whiteboard, with long red flames. 'But the sun wouldn't move, it just burned the earth, so in the end, all the gods jumped into the flames to get it moving again, which was nice of them, because if they hadn't, we'd all have been burned to a crisp.'

Henry goes slightly green.

Ursula's camera beeps off.

'So – everyone – let's choose someone to represent our sun god.'

'That was nice, being chosen as the sun god,' says Henry, beaming.

'Was it?' I ask. I can't help feeling that it wasn't such a good idea; Miss Primrose looked definitely mad to me. I'm looking out for the policeman. I should have taken his name.

'My dad's got weird though,' says Henry.

'Oh?'

'Yes, after you mentioned about your mum and the beard, I watched him on purpose. He sat in the garden, put a lampshade on his head, set fire to the fence and cooked some steak and ate it all himself.' Henry sucks in a lungful of air. 'He was really bad-tempered and took Mum's rowing machine apart and set a trap for the postman, who he accused of plotting to steal the TV.'

'Really? Your dad?' Henry's dad's a builder; he's like Henry, but more brick-like.

'Oh yes, he's definitely gone...strange. Mum's a bit off as well, she seems to be learning to ride, and she's started to sing.'

'Like what?'

'Like an animal,' says Henry. 'Like a cow, if a cow could sing.' He raises an eyebrow. 'It's not very relaxing.'

I look towards the entrance again. No policeman, but something else catches my eye, on the climbing wall. 'What's that?'

Ursula's camera whirrs and I'm guessing she's already zoomed in.

'It's fluffy,' says Henry. 'Probably one of the little kids' cuddlies. I'll get it down for them.'

We stand at the bottom. I'd have to climb to reach it, but Henry's much taller. He reaches up and tips it forward.

It's Tiny Tim, the reception class teddy. He falls face down on the safety grass and I turn him over. Behind me, a little girl screams.

Tiny Tim's glass eyes stare blankly up at the sky. His

arms lie broken on either side. The fur on his chest flaps open, revealing a raw hole in the stuffing.

He's been murdered.

His heart's gone.

His voice has gone.

His growler's been stolen.

Chapter 7

The policeman appears just before PE and just after Henry's buried Tiny Tim in the sandpit. He stands to the side of the playground and watches us. I put up my hand to speak to him, but Mr Dent's in no mood to let me off. He's wearing a tennis skirt over very tiny shorts and nothing else. Not even any trainers.

'Onto the pitch, let's have a quick once around.'

We stumble into a line and jog slowly round the football pitch. Mr Dent thunders up and down beside us. We pass the goal, and Henry points at it, raising his eyebrows. The crossbar's gone, and one of the side posts seems to have been carved.

A totem pole?

'Come on, you lot,' shouts Mr Dent, bouncing from one foot to the other. He runs off the football pitch and back into the school yard. We follow, all at different speeds.

Ricky's at the front. He's got white shorts on and his little skinny legs show up as blue next to the white. I notice because Mr Dent's legs are dark brown, as if every bottle of instant tan in the town has found its way onto his skin.

'Halt!' he shouts. Gratefully, I stop and suck in a few mouthfuls of air. 'Right, line up.'

Henry pushes himself in next to me. Ricky bounces up and down at one end, and the rest of the class forms a sort of line. It's a line in the same way that a 'W' is a line. A look of extreme irritation crosses Mr Dent's face.

'A line. What's a line? Boys?'

Henry sticks up his hand.

'Yes – Waters?'

'It's a thing that goes straight between two points, or maybe it's a line that joins point A and point B – or would it...'

'Yes, get on with it then.'

We try again. This time it's more of an 'S'.

Mr Dent's not normally scary, but today he's got a wild look in his eye, like we're not children. It's as if he sees us as something else. It worries me because it looks like

Mum and Miss Primrose. I look over to the policeman. He's leaning on the fence, watching the girls dance around a stack of road cones, and tapping his foot out of time to the thumpy bird calls floating out of the CD player balanced on the staffroom window.

'Two lines,' barks Mr Dent, and unlocks the PE cupboard. We do better this time, although I wish I was standing in the back row.

'Catch,' he shouts, throwing blue swimming floats at us. 'Come on, quick! One each.'

I grab one, only slightly gnawed, and hold it to my chest. Surely he's not thinking of taking us swimming. It's freezing and there isn't time…and we haven't got our swimming kits; we do swimming in the autumn term.

'Sir, Mr Dent, sir?' says Ricky. putting up his hand. 'Mum says I can't go swimming at the moment, because of my ears.'

Mr Dent turns and glares.

'Swimming? Who said anything about swimming?'

A minute later and we're back on the football pitch, standing in four lines of six and one of five, banked together like bottles in a crate.

Mr Dent's dragged some old things from the back of

the PE cupboard. A white pointy-ended pole, a boxing helmet and a really heavy metal disc. Ricky's carrying the disc, but he can hardly lift it above his knees.

I get to carry the boxing helmet. It's old and crunchy and hasn't been on anyone's head for a long time. I can't imagine why Mr Dent wants it.

He holds his hand out. 'Helmet, Sam.' I pass it, and he pulls it over his sandy, stubbly hair. The straps are too short and they crack as he does up the buckle. It's a squeeze, but he manages it.

He looks like someone wearing a sandal on their head.

'Right, boys, close ranks.'

We shuffle, and once again I wish I was standing in the back row. He pulls the people on the sides into the middle, until we're packed together like sardines.

'Sir?' says Henry.

Mr Dent glares at him. 'Ever thrown a javelin? Boy?'

'Yes, Mr Dent, sir,' says Henry. 'On sports day, the foam ones.'

'Foam ones!' Mr Dent laughs. 'They're not javelins! They're marshmallows. This, boy, this, is a javelin.' Mr Dent throws the white pointy stick over our heads and it buries itself inches deep in the grass, vibrating along its whole length. We turn and stare.

'Looks fun,' says Ricky.

No one else looks much like it's fun. Most people look scared and Will's bottom lip's wobbling.

'So, ever heard of a turtle as a means of defence, eh?'

I imagine the terrapins at the zoo and wonder if they could defend themselves against Mr Dent.

'Raise your shields!' he cries.

No one moves.

'Your shields, boys.' He grabs the polystyrene float from Henry's hands. 'These.'

I put my feeble float between myself and the sky. Henry does the same, although because he's so much taller, there's a gap.

Mr Dent walks behind us and pulls the javelin out of the grass.

'Defend yourselves!' he shouts, walking back round to the front. We pull closer together.

He trots out from the football pitch, taking the javelin, then almost without looking, he turns on his heel and launches the javelin straight towards us.

Only Will doesn't break rank. The rest of us scatter to the sides and the javelin quivers to a halt in the turf right next to his ankle.

Chapter 8

'So what seems to be the matter, boys?' The policeman takes off his jacket and slings it over his shoulder.

'Didn't you see that?' squeals Henry. 'It was attempted murder.'

'Oh – that's a bit strong, he was just teaching you the basics of...' The policeman looks vague. 'Hostile engagement.'

'And did you see Miss Primrose?' I say, pointing towards the pile of road cones. 'You could see she was behaving strangely, couldn't you? And those bird noises – they weren't proper music.'

'Let's not jump to conclusions,' says the policeman, tilting his head from side to side as if examining all the options. 'Let's see what all the evidence brings.' He pats me on the head as if I was a dog.

Mr Dent comes over and he and the policeman shake hands in a complicated way that seems to involve standing on one leg and hopping. 'Afternoonus,' says Mr Dent.

'Ave,' says the policeman, his hand drifting up into a Roman salute.

I look up at his eyes. For a second I see something worrying, then he smiles, and drops his arm. 'I'll pop round to your house after school, then, lad. About five, if that's all right? Have a look at these Egyptians for you.'

Yesterday's digger has cut a wide circle in the turf where the cricket pitch ought to be. Instead of twenty metres of short grass, there's half a ring of huge pieces of concrete. At the side, more giant lumps of concrete lie in a heap.

'What have they done?' says Henry. 'They've completely wrecked the pitch. 'We've got our first under-thirteens match at Easter, it'll never be ready by then, and what's all this stone for? It's a catastrophe.'

'Perfect,' says Ursula. 'It's a post-apocalyptic dystopian future landscape. It would make a brilliant film set. Tell you what, Sam, we could start on *Werewolves of the Windy Planet*.'

'Are you making a film?' asks Henry.

'Not now,' I say, 'I've got to get home.'

'And not with you,' says Ursula, stomping off through the concrete stones. She stops and stares. 'That's Queen Victoria, isn't it?' she calls, pointing. I look to see. She's right. The lumps of concrete aren't concrete at all. The statue of Queen Victoria from the Town Hall is embedded in the cricket pitch. Head first. The bottom of her chair is pointing up at the sky with a whopping great plinth at the top.

I look at the others. Lord Nelson's arrived from the park. A man on a horse from the station, a road barrier and the person who invented the coffee machine are planted alongside. By their side lie two random bollards, a modern sculpture and Isambard Kingdom Brunel.

This is by far the weirdest thing I have seen yet.

'We must film here,' she says. 'It's an unmissable opportunity. Tonight, there's a full moon. It couldn't be better.'

'With Henry,' I say quietly.

'What?' says Ursula. 'But —'

'With Henry; Henry has to be part of it too,' I say.

Ursula steps forward as if to slap me.

'Thanks, Sam,' says Henry, coming closer, putting himself between me and Ursula. 'And can I bring Lucy?'

'Lucy?' asks Ursula. 'Who is she — another hideous member of your hideous family?'

'My goat,' says Henry.

'Goat?' says Ursula. 'Did I hear you right?'

'Since when have you had a goat?' I ask.

'Since Halloween. My auntie left her to me.'

Ursula stares at him. 'You're going to bring a goat on a film set?'

Henry nods. He's deep purple now.

'Why not?' I say. 'Perhaps the werewolf eats goats?'

Ursula gives me one of her stares. 'Are you serious?'

Henry shuffles his feet.

'Why can't he bring a goat?'

'It's so unprofessional.'

I look at the floor. 'Ursula,' I mutter.

Ursula makes a movement that might be someone stamping their foot. 'Very well. Lucy can come. And you can use your imagination over costumes. So, here, six o'clock, and we'll get some of this down and done.'

'What, in the dark?' says Henry.

'Yeah,' says Ursula. 'You don't have to come.'

Henry shakes his head. 'No,' he says. 'This evening's great. Whatever you say.'

Chapter 9

Henry runs with me along the side of the cricket pitch.

'I can't believe they've done that – I mean, who would vandalise a beautiful pitch like that? I was hoping to be the opening batsman. No chance now, it'll be called off.'

I think of Mum and Miss Primrose and Mr Dent. Any of them would be capable of it at the moment.

'Sorry, Henry. It's a shame,' I say, kicking through a mess of crumbled polystyrene surrounding a half-carved polystyrene torso.

'And Ursula, is she always that rude?' Henry shakes his head. 'I could have thumped her – although of course I wouldn't thump a girl, but really.'

I can see him blinking back tears.

'She's rude to me too,' I say. 'In fact she's almost never not rude.'

'Yeah, but she was rudest to me,' says Henry, swallowing. He's right. She was much nastier to him; it's as if she's got no feelings while he's got loads. 'Thanks for standing up for me, Sam.'

'S'all right,' I mutter. 'Sometimes, she's just...' I run through the millions of words I could use to describe her. '...impossible.'

We pause for breath; I lean down with my hands on my knees, and pant. A strange strangled sound floats across the common. 'Someone in trouble?' asks Henry.

I focus on the distant trees, but I can't really see anything. 'I think it's an instrument. A horn?'

We listen. It reminds me of the music in Dad's car, and the tape that Miss Primrose inflicted on the girls. Not really music at all.

'Do we need tinfoil? For the movie?' he asks, pointing at the Grocery Basket Ever Open Convenience Store, across the road.

'Yeah,' I say. 'But I haven't got any money.'

'I have,' says Henry. 'I'll pay.'

I hate to take advantage of Henry; just because everyone else does doesn't mean I should too, but we always use shed-loads of tinfoil to make Ursula's films. That and Derf guns.

'That would be kind,' I say.

'No probs,' says Henry, stopping outside the Grocery Basket and peering in through the open door. Normally, Mrs Mytych is busy sorting the shelves, but today she's nowhere to be seen.

We search for the tinfoil, and pick up three bumper family turkey-sized rolls. Henry puts a packet of mints on the counter along with the tinfoil and two banknotes and we wait.

There's rustling behind the counter, and Mrs Mytych's eyes appear over the top. She's wearing a motorbike helmet and holding a long wooden stick. She looks from side to side, studying the rest of the shop, and shoots a glance out of the door. She sighs and stands up, ringing the rolls of tinfoil through the till and reaching out for Henry's money.

'Just you boys?'

'Yes,' I say.

'No…' she begins, opening her battered Polish/English dictionary to find the words, '…grown-up?'

'Are you all right, Mrs Mytych?' asks Henry.

She leans forward, her bike helmet almost touching the counter. 'I is OK. But boys, be careful. The world is upside down here,' she says. 'They are doing fancy dress.' She points out of the window towards the cricket pitch.

'Right you are,' says Henry, offering me and Mrs Mytych a mint.

I take one, stuff the tinfoil into my backpack and we leave the shop, running.

I slip in through our front door and catch an odd smell, chemical, like petrol stations.

That and coffee.

I don't think the policeman could have been; it's only ten to five.

In the sitting room, Marcus is shooting things on the TV. But nothing else looks at all like it did last week. The sofa's gone; so have all the lights. Loose cables hang from the walls, torches burn on the mantelpiece, Finn appears dressed in a towel and socks, eating more chocolate. Dad's sitting in the chair he took from the museum, holding a pair of walking sticks across his chest.

'Hi, Sam,' he says. 'Shoes off in my presence.'

Marcus rolls his eyes at me and points at his bare feet, so I take off my shoes and socks.

'Hi, Dad,' I say, going upstairs to my bedroom. I close the door and lean against the inside, trying not to panic, but even my room's changed.

Where my pillow and my rocket ship duvet should be,

is half a wooden salad bowl, and nothing else. The sheet and the mattress have gone too.

'Sam, my revered second son,' says Mum, stepping into the bedroom, clutching a large mug and a carrier bag.

'Mum, where's everything gone? Where's my pillow?'

'Pillow?' She looks at me oddly. 'You mean the filthy bag of feathers?' She pulls a sheet of blue sacking from the carrier bag and lays it on the bed.

I wouldn't have called my pillow filthy, but she's probably right. If you looked under a microscope, there's probably a universe of bugs living in there. Nothing compared to Marcus's though.

'Yes?'

She points at the wooden bowl. 'This, oh my revered son, is a head rest. Much cleaner. And more in keeping.'

'In keeping with what?' I say. But Mum's already heading out of the room, leaving a burning oil lamp on the floor as she goes.

Apart from anything else, it's only a matter of time before the house burns down.

BAM!

I stick my head out of the window.

BAM!

Outside on the street, is a thing like a catapult. It's

mostly made of wooden pallets and an old Mini, and surrounded by thickset men with unusually brown legs. The rugby club? Only they're not really the rugby club because they're all wearing skirts, or kind of skirts. They've fired a load of rubbish in carrier bags at our front door.

Leading them is the policeman; he's wearing his uniform with a skirt on top.

'What on earth?' I shout down to them.

'Ah – lad,' says the policeman, putting his hand up to the others. 'Come to sort out your Egyptians.'

I race down and open the door. The policeman's got that distant look in his eyes. 'Why've you brought that with you?' I ask, pointing at the catapult.

He picks his way over the rubbish. 'Always does to be prepared,' he says. 'Now – let's have a look at them.'

I'm tempted to shut the door in his face, but decide to let him in. The other men push their catapult on down the street, looking for another house to attack.

He stops in front of Dad. 'Ave!' he says, raising his arm in salute.

Dad leaps to his feet and waves a walking stick in the air like a propeller. 'Out!' he shouts. 'Out of my house! Vandal! Colonialist! Roman!'

I stare at the policeman. He'll arrest Dad for sure now, won't he?

'Now, now, sir, no need to talk to me like that, let's be civilised...'

But he doesn't get a chance to be civilised, because Mum appears behind him with a short plank of wood and brings it down on his head.

The policeman folds to the floor.

'MUM!' I shout. 'What've you done?'

'She has most excellently defeated the Roman,' says Dad, clapping his hands. 'Now we will have a slave; top work, my queen.'

Mum does a kind of bow, picks up the policeman's legs and drags him out of the French windows. I follow, just in time to rescue his head from a pile of cement.

'But, Mum, he's a policeman, you can't do this, you'll be in real trouble.'

Mum drops his feet, and ties his hands together with washing line. 'Fear not, esteemed second son of Lloyd, this is the way of the pharaohs.'

I stand, letting the policeman's head fall gently back to the ground, and look around.

Now I'm out here, I can see what they're doing. They're building a pyramid. An Egyptian one. It's actually very good; there are no lumps of mortar sticking out of the joins. It's completely smooth.

'Second son,' says Dad, behind me, switching on the cement mixer. 'Behold the great pyramid of Lloyd.'

'Dad?' I say.

'We have built this in anticipation of our deaths, and secured it against the lowly tomb robbers of the desert. See here, the secret of the tombs.'

He points to a tiny slit cut in the side of the pyramid.

'In there?'

'Oh yes, second son, we will fit, one after the other, and be sealed inside; forever. Buried properly according to the laws of the pharaohs.' I can't see his face properly, but he doesn't sound like he's joking.

Dad shovels more sand into the cement mixer.

'So are you thinking of dying sometime soon?' I ask, as Mum ties the policeman's feet together with his boot-laces.

'The moon.' Dad points at the sky. 'She is nearly at the zenith. When she is, the gods will take her away, and then it is foretold that I, Lloyd the first, shall die, and in my place shall rule Lloyd the second.'

'Marcus?'

'And under his reign, the crops will prosper and the

famines will cease. This...' He points at next door's green-house. 'All this will be gone and the desert will return.'

'And I will die too, oh second son,' says Mum, cheerfully. 'So you will need to know how to bury according to the rules of the pharaohs.'

'Will I? Couldn't Marcus do it?'

'He will be taking on the mantle of kingship, you will be his priest. Come, follow.'

Mum opens the kitchen door. Inside, the preserving pan's bubbling on the gas and the room's full of noxious smoke.

Some deep memory jumps into my mind. When I was Finn's age, we must have gone to the museum for a 'hands-on exploration day'. Somebody was there making something that smelled just like this stuff. He had a little gas burner, and a vat of stinky chemicals. He talked about salts, and preserving things.

Embalming fluid.

Yikes!

'You empty the organs into the canopic jars.' She points at the coffee, tea and sugar pots. 'And you will stopper the orifices...'

'Mum! Stop! I'm Sam, I'm eleven. I'm not a high priest. I play with Derf guns and make things out of cardboard.'

She blinks.

'I haven't the faintest idea about mummification, or embalming or any of that stuff.'

For a moment, something shines in her eye, a little fragment of Mum, but it clouds over and she says, 'You will learn.'

Chapter 10

The sky's darkening. An orange moon hangs low over the houses amidst early-evening stars. The town's eerily quiet except for the squeak of Finn's old pushchair.

I've brought it with me to carry everything I own. On top of my clothes, I've balanced two loaded Derf guns. One of them is the Derf Super Blaster; it can fire a superb thirty-six rounds per minute. I'm not going anywhere without that at the moment. I also have a sleeping bag, six oranges and a grapefruit, and as an afterthought all the hairy things I could find, like the bathmat and Dad's dressing gown. If we don't use them for filming *Werewolf* then I could always sleep under them. Last of all I took the empty cardboard washing-machine box from behind the wheelie bin. It can either be the lunar module, or my new home, depending on how things work out.

I think I've actually run away from home. It seems safer to sleep out on the common in the washing-machine box, eating grapefruit, than to risk my bedroom and my parents.

I try to remember when it started. The beard was the first obvious thing. But Dad ordered a load of insulation blocks about two weeks ago. The same insulation blocks that he's now sawing in half and turning into a pyramid.

Perhaps that was it. Perhaps it was already happening but I didn't spot it.

But Miss Primrose didn't start then, surely. Although she did bring in those old pillows at least a week before the wetsuit.

'Woooooooooaaaaaaaaaah!'

What was that?

'Yeeeeooooooooooowww!'

I dive over a low wall into a garden, but I can't bring the pushchair, and have to leave it on the other side.

Feet, and I mean bare feet, slap on the pavement, but there's also a clacky sound, like someone in heels.

'Woo,' says a high voice. A woman.

I can hear someone sniffing. The sniffing gets closer, and closer. I crouch.

'Ha!' the woman shouts, grabbing my hair.

'Yow!' I scream.

'Urgh!' she cries, and yanks my hair until I'm standing.

Four people stand behind her. One of them is the school secretary. She's gnawing on a bone. She looks crazed. They're all dressed in fur of one sort or another. Fur?

Struggling on the end of the woman's hand I reach for the pushchair, wrench open my backpack, pull out Dad's furry brown dressing gown and put it on.

The hair yank woman stares at me, her brows furrowing.

I put the towelling bathmat over my shoulders.

'Ooohhhw,' says Hair Yank, dropping me and standing back.

'Aah,' says one of the men; he's wearing a stupidly small fox fur round his neck, like old ladies in detective programmes.

'Ug,' says another, who's so tall I can't see his face properly.

Hair Yank grabs me by the hand and, helped by the school secretary, hauls me over the wall. I'm not sure, but Hair Yank looks awfully like the woman that works in the hairdresser's. The woman I saw painting a deer on the outside of her house. In every way Stone Age except for the nail varnish and the high heels.

They push me along the pavement, while I push the pushchair. When we reach the common, they caper across to the statue ring. For a second I'm free, but the tall man stops about ten feet from me, comes back, picks me up and carries me over to the statue Stonehenge. He puts me down and leans on my shoulders, clamping me to the ground.

Curiously, although he's dressed as an ancient Briton of some sort, he smells of aftershave.

'Urghghg!' the man with the dead animal round his neck shouts, pointing at the moon.

The last stones in the ring have been slipped into place since we were here earlier. But the modern statue's lying on its side in the middle like an altar.

'Baaaaa.' What's that? It sounds almost like a sheep. But it could be a goat.

Please let it be a goat.

'Shhhhhh.' Now that, definitely, sounds like Henry.

I look around. There's no actual sign of Henry and his goat, but he must be there. There are plenty of stones to hide behind. My guard stops and sniffs the air as if he can smell food but then, obviously not quite Stone Age enough to spot a goat in the dark, turns and joins the others.

My captors look very serious. One of the men's got a National Trust tea towel on his head and a set of letter beads around his neck and they all look to him. He looks up at the moon and then points at a bright star.

'Ulph,' he says. 'Ulph.'

The tall man lets go of me, and joins the others. They kneel in a semicircle around the stone, facing the tea-towel man. From under his dressing gown, he takes something long and silver that glints in the moonlight. A paperknife?

I hold my breath, moving to the back, hoping no one will notice me leave. If I take a couple of steps to my right, I can hide behind Queen Victoria.

Something squeaks behind the stones. It doesn't sound like a goat, but it does sound like a pushchair.

I look around. The pushchair's moved from where I left it. That means Henry must be nearby.

Phew.

'Woooooaaghghghghg,' says Tea-towel Man, and they all start to hum.

'Mmmmmmmmmmmmmmmm, mmmmmmmmmmmmm.'

I take a step to the side and slip behind Queen Victoria.

'Mmmmmmmmm, mmmmmmmm.'

Tea-towel Man's got his eyes closed, but he's holding his paperknife up to the moon.

'Mmmmmm, mmmm.'

'Pst, Sam.' It's Henry's voice, but I can't see him. 'Here,' he whispers. 'By Nelson.'

I look for the tallest stone, and there, about a metre

above the foot, well, the head in Nelson's case, is an odd, glowing lump. It beckons.

I drop to my knees and crawl towards it.

'WHOA!' screams Hair Yank and suddenly I'm whisked backwards.

'Help!' I shout.

'Sam!' shouts Henry, but the worshippers take no notice.

Hair Yank drags me towards the altar, and Fox Fur and Tall Man grab my wrists. 'Help!' I shout more loudly, and for a second there's a flash of recognition in Tall Man's eyes, like he might really be a human being.

'Put me down,' I yell, and the first Derf pellet whizzes across my nose, thudding into Hair Yank's cheek.

'Yow!' she squeals, and I wriggle and kick, but between the three of them they have no trouble lifting me off the ground and hoisting me above their heads. The ground seems a long way away now.

Another pellet thwacks into the tall man on my right. 'Yip!' he says, letting go of my foot. I squirm and the other two struggle to hold me, until I'm almost on ground level again. I lash out with my free leg, and catch Fox Fur hard on the ribs.

'Urgh!' he grunts, his hands slipping.

A third dart ricochets from the altar and pings into the

chin of the man with the tea towel. 'What?' he says, staring around himself like he's just woken up.

There's a clicking sound and a hail of purple pellets crashes into the group.

The last two left holding me finally let go, and I thump onto the ground.

A strange figure appears at the edge of the group; it's got a silver ball for a head and two faintly glowing light bulbs strapped on the side, and it's wearing the washing machine box. Out of the door pokes the Derf Super Blaster, firing thirty-six pellets a minute. The figure doesn't move well, blundering into the stones, hampered by a goat tied to the side. From the washing machine box come peals of giggles, and the goat obviously wants to be somewhere else, none of which helps the figure's aim because the pellets are hitting everyone, including me. But I don't mind; I'm very glad to be shot – it's far better than being dangled in the air.

'I don't understand,' says Hair Yank, gazing at her nail varnish.

'Run!' yells Ursula from somewhere in the outer darkness.

Waiting for the hand on my collar again, I tack through the stones, skimming over the scraped turf, running for my life. Away in the dark someone else is running. It must be Ursula. And we head for the deep shadow of the cricket pavilion.

'Yee ha!' shouts Henry, skidding to a heavy halt beside me, accompanied by the sound of tearing cardboard and a squeal from the goat. 'Now that was fun,' he says, ripping the glowing helmet from his head.

'Fun?' I say. 'What do you suppose they were thinking of doing with that altar?'

'Turning you into Sam burgers, that's what I think,' says Henry, stroking the goat between the ears. 'Don't you, Lucy?'

Ursula splutters. 'Don't be stupid, Henry, they weren't going to harm Sam. They're just playing around.' She gets to her feet. 'This is the most boring town in twenty-first century Britain. There is absolutely no chance of human sacrifice here.'

Chapter 11

The washing-machine box is cramped and cold, and actually a horrible place to spend the night, but I parked myself next to some other cardboard boxes, so I'm hoping that no one'll notice me. Things rustle all around, in and out of the boxes, creeping through the undergrowth. Other things howl and grunt; I can't tell if they're animal or human.

At what must be about five o'clock, I give up and pull on my balaclava. It makes me feel safer. Leaving almost everything in the washing-machine box, I eat an orange and fill my backpack with Derf guns.

I creep towards the ring of statues.

The people who were there last night have gone, but my Derf pellets are still lying on the ground, so I pick them up and reload. I feel very slightly safer, and watch as the sun comes up over Isambard Kingdom Brunel.

I wander round to Ursula's house. Outside the hospital I pass three melons and a collection of footballs skewered on a Belisha beacon. There's something nasty about it; somehow they remind me of heads. A little further on, a flock of sheep grazes in the garden centre, surrounding a small round hut hung with shoes; but when I reach Ursula's road, it all looks normal. Why have her parents not built a pyramid? Why is she not in training to be a high priestess?

I feel a curious mixture of pride and fear as I remember Mum's words.

But orifices? Yuk.

I chuck a fir cone at Ursula's window and her face appears instantly. She looks white, and maybe scared.

A second later and she's standing fully dressed outside the front of her house.

'Trojans,' she mutters. 'They've turned into Trojans. They're getting ready to fight the Greeks from the takeaway, but the Greeks from the takeaway aren't interested and have barricaded themselves into their shop.' She puts her hands over her ears. 'It's not nice, I wish they'd stop. I've hardly slept – Mum's throwing pots on the old record player, she'll blow herself up soon.'

Perhaps being an Egyptian priest isn't so bad.

'What's the time? Are we going to school?' asks Ursula, looking in her camera case.

'To see what Miss Primrose is up to?'

Ursula checks her camera. 'Maybe not; anyway, it's only five to six'

I hand her a Derf gun. 'Let's go and find Henry,' I say.

'Henry? Why? We've only just got rid of him.'

'Who fired that first shot last night?'

'Henry did.'

'Exactly,' I say.

We sit in Henry's garage, watching his dad, Genghis Khan, attacking the neighbour, Attila the Hun, with a bicycle pump. Ursula's filming it through the open door and Henry's peeling an orange.

The last time I came to Henry's house, it was all spick and span. This time, it's draped with stinky animal skins and I can see where they've been cooking because there's a pile of charcoal dotted with burned supermarket ready meals in the driveway.

'So, I think we'd all say, there's something really wrong,' says Ursula.

'Ursula?' I say. 'Have you only just noticed?'

She sticks her tongue out at me, while Henry clicks Derf pellets into the gun.

'What about your sisters?' I ask Henry. 'Are they weird too?'

'You can't tell with the twins,' he says. 'They're always peculiar. They've shut themselves into their bedroom; been there for hours. They're living on Easter eggs and candy pigs they stole from Mum's cupboard.'

'Marcus's fine. But Finn's not.' Mum didn't say what was going to happen to Finn. Perhaps he gets to be a farmer or something harmless. I hope I'm not expected to mummify him, I wouldn't want to go anywhere near his 'orifices'.

'They were Stone Age last night,' says Henry.

'Actually they weren't,' says Ursula. 'I think you'll find they were Bronze or even Iron Age.'

'Surely not,' he says, going a slightly darker shade of brick. 'They built in stone.'

'Yes, but they had metal tools.' Ursula looks smug.

Henry glares at Ursula. I can't imagine how irritating it must be living with two identical Ursulas. Poor Henry. At least Marcus is mostly silent except for things dying on screen, and Finn mostly goes to bed in the evenings.

'Someone should do something about it,' says Henry. 'Like the army – perhaps we should call the army?'

'I dare you to make the call,' says Ursula. '"Hello, my dad thinks he's Genghis Khan, and he's wearing a lamp-shade on his head and attacking the neighbour with a bicycle pump, and my friend's dad's building a pyramid."' Ursula stares at him. 'Well – go on, then.'

Henry flushes.

'Anyway,' I say, ignoring Ursula. 'I tried the police. My mum ended up imprisoning the policeman. She's turning him into a slave.'

'Do you mean it's up to us?' asks Henry, a note of excitement in his voice.

Ursula does a long theatrical sigh.

'Yes, Henry, I do,' I say, turning away so that I can't see Ursula rolling her eyes at me. 'So, my family's Egyptian, yours are Mongols, Henry, and Ursula's are Trojans.' They nod. 'The people last night were Stone Age/Iron Age/ Bronze Age.'

'Mr Dent's Roman,' says Henry.

'Or Greek?' says Ursula.

'And what about Miss Primrose?'

Henry chews his lip. 'Miss Primrose is an Aztec, she told us.'

We sit silently listening to the screaming from the fight outside. Without looking, it sounds like Henry's dad's winning.

'So it's all to do with history?' says Henry, pulling the garage door shut, so that we can't actually see the violence.

Ursula sighs and films a small square on the wall.

'No, Henry, you're right, it is all to do with history,' I say. 'They've all gone historical.'

'It's a government plot,' says Ursula, 'To stop us noticing the state of the nation, since we're all too busy fighting each other.'

'But we're not all fighting,' says Henry. 'I reckon it's an alien invasion. Some people have been sent mad so that the rest of us are too busy to notice the spaceship landing on the roof.'

'Henry,' says Ursula. 'That is obviously, completely stupid.'

We sit listening to the screams from outside; they're becoming more ferocious.

'Do you think those are authentic Mongol screams?' I ask.

'They could be Hunnish,' says Henry, listening. 'Dad's almost certainly going to win. He's twice the size of Attila the Hun.'

'Who was more vicious?' I ask.

Henry shrugs.

'A visit to the museum, then,' says Ursula.

We both stare at her.

'History? The past? The museum is the grand repository of the past in this concrete wasteland. And we, obviously, know nothing.'

'You mean,' I say, 'that we're going to go to the museum, on purpose?'

'Anyone got any better ideas?' asks Ursula.

Chapter 12

I have to steal the keys, of course, and the other two don't come with me, but using Henry's bike, I make it home. I pedal fast between the two halves of a Trojan horse that's growing out of corrugated iron behind the Greek takeaway, and skirt around the back of our house. No one sees me; Marcus is probably still asleep, and the cement mixer's grinding away in the back garden, so I pocket the keys and belt back to the museum, passing a new forge that's suddenly appeared on the high street. I find Henry and Ursula lurking outside the museum cafe. All the tables have been pushed together in the middle of the room. A giant chocolate fountain sits on the central table, hot dark chocolate coursing down the sides, filling the room and the street with a fantastic smell.

'Oh wow, look at that,' I say.

'Yeah,' says Henry. 'We tried to get close, dip in a piece of banana, but we couldn't get past her.' He points at a woman with a tattooed face.

'Fair enough,' I say. 'But I could kill for some breakfast.'

We unlock the doors of the museum, slip inside and lock them behind us. Our feet echo on the floor. All the interactive screens are blank and silent.

'Whhhhhhhooooooooooooooooo,' calls Ursula.

'Whhhooooooooooo,' says the museum echo.

'Creepy,' whispers Henry.

We pad forward past the gift shop and something hums behind us. The ice-cream freezer. 'Yay!' I say, and the echo answers me.

'Yaaaaay.'

I yank open the lid and rummage inside.

'Should we leave some money?' asks Henry.

'I don't –' I begin.

'No,' says Ursula, wrapping her lips round a strawberry split chocolate sparkle. Henry raises his eyebrows and picks up a leaflet from a stand.

'Hey, look at this,' he says. 'FLAP! Film from Local Artists Prize.'

'What?' says Ursula, grabbing it from Henry. 'Age groups: Adult, 14–19 and 9–13. Yay – perfect!' She follows us into the Egyptian Hall. 'It's going to be judged by David Pringle, the Hollywood director −'

'Are you going to enter?'

Ursula's eyes widen but she doesn't look away from the leaflet. 'Am I going to enter? Just the idea that David Pringle might watch one of my movies…is so…so…Of course, Sam, we're going to enter. ' She pulls her face into a tragic mask. 'It gives me a *raison d'être!*'

While I wonder what a raisin detre is, I peer into the shiny new cases. Some of them now appear empty. Is that Dad's doing? Perhaps it's just as well we've taken the keys. Our footsteps ring in the empty hall and I keep expecting someone with a walkie-talkie to jump out at us and tell us to step away from the exhibits.

Ursula stops in front of the coffin of Homotep III. She's reading the leaflet again.

Henry reads the label on the case. '*Married at eight to a woman of thirty-two, Homotep's short rule was marked by famine and disaster.* Oh yes,' he says. 'There were famines, weren't there? Weren't there seven plagues too? The first one was the locusts, or was it the −'

Ursula cuts him off, taking her camera out of the bag and filming us. 'Let's keep moving, I'd like to get this over and done with.'

At the end of the hall, she stops by a door that says STAFF ONLY. 'So, who's going through there, then?' she asks.

'You?' says Henry, quietly, looking at her.

'We should, I suppose,' I say, sidling up to the door and giving it a nudge. It swings wide, crashing open against the wall, showing a flight of stairs disappearing into darkness.

'C'mon, you two,' she says, although she doesn't move. To be fair, she's holding the camera and they're only stairs, and the museum's empty; it's just that I don't much fancy finding a mummy standing in a cupboard or anything like that, but I step forward and pretend that I don't care.

I march to the bottom of the stairs in darkness and stand, waiting for my eyes to get used to it. To my left, the first door. I turn the handle, pull open the door and something falls against me.

'Aaarghghgh!' I leap backwards and the lights suddenly come on to show that I've been attacked by a coat.

'Come on, silly,' says Ursula, striding to the end of the corridor. 'Try that one.'

This door hums. I hesitate before pushing my way in, and it's Henry who goes first, while I fumble for the light switch. It's a large bunker. The humming comes from a noisy machine that hangs over the long benches running along the walls. It might be something to control the temperature, or the humidity, or just get rid of the dust, because everything in here is dusty. The room feels like a massive ancient kitchen, without a cooker, but with a sink, and it's cold in here, really cold. On the counter where you might prepare the vegetables, there's a mummy. It's not so scary, because it's lying down, with some of its bandages unwrapped to show the ancient skin underneath. It looks like someone cooked it, then peeled back the coverings to see how well done it was, like a burned jacket potato, and then covered it in dust.

'Yuk,' says Henry. Ursula's camera whines behind me.

Scattered alongside the mummy are plastic takeaway tubs filled with stuff; heaps of crumbly things that might be fragments of human bodies, or worse. They're littered with tiny white numbered labels, as if someone's going to come back and sort them out. At the end of the counter is a large red leather book.

'So, what is all this...?' says Henry, prodding a plastic pot heaped with grey sponge.

I shrug.

'I suspect,' says Ursula, from behind the camera, 'these are the things that used to be in the cases out at the front, that your dad said they weren't sure about.'

'Could be,' I say, opening the red book. It has lines of neat black handwriting, a number, then a description, running for page after page. 'Give me a number, Henry.'

'Er – E.G.P. 3894 – 27, any good?'

I run my finger down the pages. There's a whole column devoted to EGP and eventually I find number 27. '*Egyptian bread,*' I say. '*From the tomb of Rameses the second, bought by Lady Oswald Fletcher in Cairo in June 1860. Unverified.*'

Henry gazes into the plastic box.

'And this?' asks Ursula, rattling another box.

'*Corn, from Titech…I can't read it, in Mexico, said to be Aztec. Given by Archibald Knee, 1956. Unverified.*'

'Fancy that,' says Henry. 'If this really is Egyptian bread, then it's at least two thousand years old.'

We all peer at it. It doesn't look very much like bread. It looks more like that stuff flower arrangers use.

'Hmmm,' says Ursula. 'Not very helpful. Come on, let's have a look for the Aztecs, and pick up another ice lolly on the way.' She swings out through the door and marches back along the corridor.

We follow, but I leave the light on; I don't like to think of that mummy lying there in the dark.

Chapter 13

The Aztecs, it turns out, are a pretty nasty bunch. Miss Primrose told us about the sun thing, but she didn't tell the full story about the sun thing. Apparently, the Aztecs were under the impression that if they didn't give shedloads of human hearts as a present to the sun, it would stop moving in the sky. There are stacks of drawings of priests dressed as gods, and gods dressed as suns and stone tablets of more priests dressed as suns. It's bewildering, and I wish Dad was here to explain it all, because I can't work out who is really who, and who is just dressed up as someone.

I stand staring at a case with a carved tablet of a figure in a headdress. It's exactly like my dream. On the back of the display is a drawing of an Aztec temple, the steps running with blood and masses of bodies lying at the bottom. One figure is obviously dressed as the sun, holding a sun disc and wearing a particularly large set of feathers.

'Nice,' says Henry. 'Which one's the sun?'

'That one,' I point at the drawing. 'Or at least, he's playing the part of the sun.'

'Do you mean the one covered in blood, lying at the bottom of the steps?' asks Henry.

I nod. 'I think so, although…I don't totally understand it.'

Henry loses all shades of brick and turns clay in colour.

'But, stupids, this is Miss Primrose,' says Ursula. 'She's not mentioned anything about this stuff.' She points at the case. 'She's far too nice, she wears fluffy white trainer socks and smells of roses. I'd be more worried about the Stone Age lot.'

'Bronze Age,' corrects Henry.

It's Ursula's turn to flush.

'I know Miss Primrose is sweet and lovely,' I say. 'But she's not shown any signs of it in the last few days, and two weeks ago, if anyone had said that my parents would build a pyramid in the garden and appoint me as a high priest, I wouldn't have believed them.'

'So?' says Ursula, tapping her foot on the floor.

'Where are the Mongol Hordes?' asks Henry.

'Over there.' Ursula points to the other end of the gallery and Henry stomps off to look at the cases. 'What are you saying, Sam?'

I point at the picture. 'Human sacrifice,' I say. 'Lots of it.'

'You're just being silly.'

'OK, well, tell me what else they do,' I say. 'Find something nice about the Aztecs. And why does Miss Primrose want a sun?'

Ursula reads all the smart labels. 'They worshipped loads of different gods, not just the sun.'

'Yes, and how did they appease them?' I ask, looking at a huge stone knife.

Ursula reads for a moment. 'OK, fair enough, more hearts. But here's one.' She jabs at a case. 'Agriculture, that was just watery little floating flower beds – that would be quite nice really.'

'Have you seen Miss Primrose building floating flower beds?'

'No,' she says. 'But then I haven't seen her rip anyone's heart out.'

A chill runs down my spine. I remember Miss Primrose sitting in the classroom, playing with the sheep noise machine; I suddenly understand where she got it from. 'Haven't you?'

'No – nice Miss Primrose, ripping out someone's heart? Of course not.'

'Think, think hard,' I say.

She stares at me. 'Not Tiny Tim? Not his growler?'

'Exactly,' I say. 'Tiny Tim; and the costume she's been wearing, I know it's made of a duvet and a wetsuit, but it's awfully like this person.' I point at a black and white engraving drawn by a Spaniard. 'Quetzalcoatl – the feathered snake god.'

'And what did he do?'

'He was the one that stood on top of the temple and ripped out the hearts.'

We stand and stare at the exhibits. Suddenly all this dry dead stuff from the past makes sense to me. These feathered hats were worn by priests; murdering priests. These curved knives were exactly the things that cut holes in the victims' chests, before the priest ripped out their hearts.

'You're actually serious about this, aren't you? You think Henry's her target?'

I think for a minute. 'I don't think she's planning on murdering the whole class; it was the way she said it, "Let's choose our sun", like we were choosing a victim. I think we chose Henry.'

'How interesting,' says Ursula as if it was a maths

problem. 'I wonder how she was planning on doing it? I mean, he's twice her size.'

'That doesn't matter. Henry's so nice, he'd never hurt a fly. He's the perfect victim. If she tells him to lie down, he'll do it – and then it'll be too late. She'll...' I rerun the day in the classroom, with the feathers drifting across the floor. Miss Primrose building the temple from school chairs, and talking about something. Something odd. What was it – something to do with the time, or the calendar?

I'm fishing about in my memory when Henry comes over, purple and anxious.

'Well, that was interesting.'

We stare at him.

'The Mongol Hordes, they played polo, charged around on little ponies.'

'Did they?' asks Ursula, looking bored.

'Do you know what they used for a ball?'

I shake my head. I don't know anything about the Mongols.

'Either the head of a prisoner – or if they didn't have one – a goat's head,' says Henry, his bottom lip wobbling.

Chapter 14

If Lucy the goat's prepared to be tied to a pushchair in the dark, she can't be that difficult to steal from under the noses of the Mongol Hordes or Henry's parents, depending on how far gone they are. Assuming she's still alive.

He says the trick with the goat is to make her believe that she thought of it, whatever it is, and that way she'll do what you want. I wonder if that would work on Ursula. Whatever happens, I'm not letting Henry out of my sight. If Miss Primrose is going to rip his heart out, then she'll have to deal with me first.

It's just reaching Henry's house that's difficult; that and persuading Ursula that it's worth rescuing a goat. 'Why are we rescuing a goat, when the ancient tribes of the world are massacring each other all over the town?'

'Why are you so worried?' I ask, looking at Ursula. It's not like her to show concern for other people.

'I'd just hate to miss it,' she says, holding up her camera.

The doors of the Parish Hall fly open as we try to pass, and the Women's Union, with saucepans on their heads and brooms in their hands, fill the street.

'Move,' I hiss at Henry, who has frozen at the sight, and we throw ourselves behind a large wheelie bin peppered with what look like broken arrow shafts. Ursula follows us.

Although I can't see very well, it's obvious that the women are furious with something; they shout and bang and crash, and form a circle, dancing one way, then the other, faster and faster, yelping and whooping. They sound as if they're about to go to war.

They stop. There's silence and I poke my head around the corner to look. They're poised, most of them with a single foot in the air, like a party of ogres. 'Onward,' someone shouts and they charge off down the alley, leaving the hall doors wide open.

We wait, listening.

Distant shouts echo through the streets. I crawl from my hiding place and gaze into the quiet hall. I'm not sure what I expected to find; there's a ring of tables, a tray of empty coffee cups, some large circles daubed on the wall in what I hope is mud, and a plate of biscuits.

Jammie Dodgers.

'Wow,' says Henry. 'Food!'

He charges in, but I stay in the doorway. Ursula hovers behind me. Something doesn't feel right.

'What is it?' says Henry, turning towards us.

'WAAAAAAAAAAAAAAAAAAHHHHHHHHHAAHAHA-HHAHAHAH!'

A fast and angry creature jumps from the rafters.

'AAAAAAAGHGH!' screams Henry, and the Jammie Dodgers fly across the room. I dive to pick them up; so does Henry.

'AAAAAAAAAAAAAAA!' we all scream.

Then the thing from the rafters picks up a chair, and we back off.

It's Mrs Mytych from the shop. She looks completely terrified. She's wearing black. A black bobble hat, black trousers and a black top, like some sort of secret agent. For a second I face her in the doorway, and then as she launches the chair, I run as hard as I can.

The chair crashes behind us on the street, but we keep on running, only we've gone the wrong way, because when we burst out of the alleyway into the square, the women are lined up against the bookshop. They look really angry. Opposite them, the rugby club have formed a square, a bit like the thing that Mr Dent wanted us to do – only neater and with bin lids.

One of the women launches a mop, but the rugby club hold firm and the mop bounces off the bin lids.

'Na na na na na,' yells one of the Romans. 'Feeblus!'

A hail of dustpans and buckets flies across the square.

'Patheticus!' yells another.

'Mr Dent,' whispers Ursula, pointing. Sure enough, Mr Dent's brown legs are lurking underneath a dustbin lid at the back. He's swapped his tennis skirt for a tunic.

The Romans fire back, rugby balls bouncing across the square, then break lines, chasing the women off in a wild screaming charge.

'Let's get out of here,' says Ursula. 'Henry, you first.'

Ponies stand in the street outside Henry's house. One of them's real, two of them are the plastic ones from the saddler's on the high street, and there's a rocking horse.

Henry puts his fingers to his lips. There's shouting and laughter, and in the front garden, a kind of tent, made from doormats and blankets.

'It's a yurt,' whispers Henry. Ursula raises an eyebrow. 'Saw it in the museum.'

We flatten ourselves against the wall and squeeze down the alleyway to the back of the house. It's blocked with heavy metal bins. Henry scrapes them over the concrete and I hold my breath waiting for someone to come outside, but the laughing and singing goes on and no one seems to notice.

We make it through to the back garden to find Lucy, the goat, lying on her back, trussed to the patio table. She sees Henry and lets out a piteous bleat.

'Oh, Lucy,' he says and steps forward, but Ursula grabs him, pointing at the glass doors and the dim shapes inside the house.

'You can't,' she whispers. 'They'll see us. We'll have to wait until dark.' She yanks him back behind the barbecue.

'But they might eat her before then,' says Henry.

'He's right,' I whisper. 'We'll have to do something before that – I mean, look, they've got her tied up, ready. It's going to happen any minute.'

At that moment, the door slides open and Henry's substantial mother steps into the garden. She's wearing a large flowered lampshade on her head, and has squeezed herself into something that might once have been a carpet.

'Are we ready? Or what?' she yells back into the house. She's carrying a bread knife.

Someone calls something to her, and she turns and goes back inside, leaving the bread knife on the table.

'Now!' I yell, springing forward and grabbing the knife. They've only tied Lucy down with bungees, but they don't cut easily.

'S'all right, Lucy darling,' says Henry, stroking Lucy's head while Ursula fiddles with a knot under the table. 'We'll have you out in a second.'

'HEY!' There's a big shout from the house, and I slice through the last strand of bungee.

'Run!' yells Ursula, and Henry picks Lucy up in his arms and we crash back past the metal dustbins, racing through the startled horses and not stopping until we reach the common.

Chapter 15

Goats don't make good house guests.

Ask any vet, they must know. I know, because Henry spends the night in my room with Lucy, hiding her from the Mongol Hordes and, although he doesn't know it, hiding himself from Miss Primrose. Although I thought I'd left home, it turns out it's the safest place to be. The town is filled with marauding historical gangs beating each other up, no place for two boys and a goat. Mum, Dad and the policeman seem quite happy building the pyramid and preparing for the afterlife.

'Your room stinks,' says Marcus. He's carried the games box and TV upstairs and is now shooting things in my bedroom because his is all soggy. The policeman irrigated it earlier; he diverted the sink outlet, and he's planted papyrus seeds in the carpet.

'Sorry,' says Henry.

BLEEEEEEAT.

Not only does Lucy stink, but she's eaten my duvet cover. 'Is there anywhere safe to put her?' I say, watching the leg of my pyjamas disappear into her mouth.

'What about the riding stables or somewhere?' says Marcus, mowing down a string of aliens with one hand and stuffing dry breakfast cereal into his mouth with the other.

'Brilliant,' says Henry. 'Come on, Sam, let's take her there.'

'Is that really any safer?' I ask.

Pwew

Pwew

Pwew

Another three aliens die on screen.

'Well, at least they'll have hay there,' says Henry.

Something pops up on the screen to tell Marcus that his friend Amos is online.

'Did you go to school yesterday?' I ask Marcus.

'Yeah, but I needn't have bothered — hang on a sec, Amos!' he yells. 'Get that Freak behind me, yeah, the one with the tendrils — yeah the Head's always been weird, but now he's convinced he's Alexander the Great. He made

us all march up and down and declared war on the girls'
school. They poured cooking oil over the fence to keep us
out, and he set fire to it.'

Pwew

'Now, Amos, now – SHOOT HIM! NO – you idiot, him,
not me.'

'Was everyone all right?' asks Henry, stroking Lucy's
nose.

Pwew

Pwew

'Yeah – but we didn't learn much, except that Alexander
the Great was bonkers. Not a lot of use as we're supposed
to be studying the Second World War.'

'Did you know,' says Henry, 'that there's supposed to be
an eclipse today?'

'That's it, that's what she said,' I say.

'Who?' asks Marcus, shooting Amos.

'Miss Primrose. So, the sun'll disappear?'

'Duh!' says Marcus.

'Not completely,' says Henry. 'It's only a partial eclipse,
but the birds'll go to roost, and it'll go dark.'

Pwew

Pwew

'So what'll happen to Miss Primrose, if the sun

disappears? Won't she try to do something to bring it back?' I ask, wondering whether I can hide Henry; if it's physically possible to hide something so big and red.

'Perhaps today's her big day,' says Henry. 'Perhaps we should go and find her, tell her about it.'

NO! I think, but say, 'I expect she already knows.'

'Hey, look at this one, he's really weird,' says Marcus, pointing at the screen. A huge green creature with fangs and red glowing eyes lumbers towards us. 'Amos – get him!'

Pwew

Pwew

Pwew

The last alien dies and Lucy swamps the floor with evil-smelling widdle.

Chapter 16

The riding stables seem deserted. Even the horses have gone, although the walls are covered in cave paintings, so perhaps the Stone Age have discovered horses; perhaps they've eaten them. We've agreed to find a safe place for Lucy, before searching out Miss Primrose.

'We need to find her,' I say. 'Before she finds us.' I stare meaningfully at Henry.

'So?' says Ursula. 'There are three of us, and she's only little, and although I've seen plenty of evidence of other civilisations, there's not a peep out of the Aztecs around the place.'

In the end, Ursula agrees that if we find Miss Primrose and wrap her in parcel tape until after the eclipse, then we can keep her and Henry safe. Ursula agrees that all methods are fair under the circumstances.

'So can I sit on her?' asks Henry, rather surprised to find that he is the probable victim of Miss Primrose's murderous intentions.

Ursula and I look at Henry's huge legs, exchange glances and decide that, yes, he can.

'This doesn't look right,' says Ursula, filming another empty loose box. 'Shouldn't there be horses here?'

'I'm not sure I want to leave Lucy,' says Henry.

'No,' I say. 'It doesn't feel good.'

The only place we haven't looked is the large barn at the end. The doors are shut while all the other doors hang open. I reach for a Derf gun and check the chamber. Fully loaded, and two clips spare.

I nod towards the barn. 'I think we should have a look in there.'

Henry leads Lucy into a small loose box on the side and ties her to the manger. It's stuffed with hay and she grabs big mouthfuls. I expect it tastes better than my pyjamas. I hand Ursula a loaded Derf gun and we tiptoe towards the barn. There's a small door at the side, so we try it first.

EEEEEEEEEEEEEKKKKKK.

For a moment, it appears empty; just a huge space, the ceiling held up by some telegraph poles, some more telegraph poles in a pile at the end, and a floor of sawdust.

And then I realise, that the floor has three small round objects in it.

Heads.

Heads?

One of them's facing us, and it's the vicar.

I can tell it's the vicar, because they've left the dog collar sticking out of the ground. He's Maria Snetter's dad, and he comes to our school all the time telling us to be good. He's got wide staring eyes and a taped-up mouth, and is nodding towards another door at the back of the barn.

'Quick,' I say, grabbing a shovel from the side. 'Dig them out.'

'Maria!' says Ursula, wrenching a length of sticking plaster from another head. 'What happened?'

'Ow!' yelps Maria, shaking her head. 'Careful — that's my face you're pulling off.' Ursula raises her eyebrows.

'But I am glad to see you,' she gabbles in time to stop Ursula from stomping away. 'It was scary, terrifying. They ambushed us at the vicarage. Dad was building a pillar on the front lawn, he was going to live up there like St Simeon Stylites, but we didn't stand a chance.' Ursula scrabbles behind her, pulling sawdust away, pushing up clouds of dust. I help, pushing the spoil heap away from the hole. 'They got Mum first, then Dad, and I tried to hide in the cellar with Amos, but they rugby-tackled me before I got there. Amos must still be in the cellar, he probably doesn't even realise anything's happened. Then they marched us here and made us dig our own holes. Dad was delighted, he said he was an early Christian martyr.'

'Didn't the early Christian martyrs come to horrible ends?' asks Ursula, reaching down Maria's back.

Maria nods. 'Exactly; Dad's gone mad — it's like the Romans were the answer to his prayers.' We dig down to Maria's shoulders; she doesn't look quite so weird, although she does look as if someone's emptied an entire guinea pig cage over her head.

'So when will they be back?' I ask, shovelling sawdust away from the hole.

'Any minute,' says Maria. 'They've gone to get the rest of the Romans, before the games.'

'Games?' asks Henry, pulling the sticky tape from Maria's dad's mouth and pawing at the sawdust like a huge puppy.

'Oh merciful Lord,' moans Maria's dad. 'The vile unchristian Romans are making us into their sport...'

'This,' says Maria, 'apparently, is the Circus Maximus. We're waiting for the lions.'

'Lions?' asks Henry, grabbing another shovel and doubling his speed.

'Yes,' says Maria. 'Mind my chin, Henry. If you can get down as far as my hands I could push myself out, but they're tied behind my back. The lions are coming, they seemed to have some in mind. They've gone off on horses to get them.'

'Can they all ride?' I ask, imagining the rugby club perched on Shetland ponies careering through the streets.

'I don't expect so,' says Henry. 'And where would they get lions from? I mean, I know there's one at the safari park but they'd never be able to catch it, and there are some mountain lions at Knarborough Park, and then I suppose there are big cats, for example…'

'Shut up, Henry,' says Ursula, reaching for the knots behind Maria's back. We yank Maria out of the ground before starting on her parents.

'Dad's going through some sort of delusion about being St Stephen, he's been rambling now for hours – is Mum OK?' asks Maria, shaking the sawdust out of her T-shirt.

'I think she's fainted,' says Henry, digging out around Maria's mum.

'Hurry,' says Ursula, and we scrabble at the ground around the vicar and his unconscious wife. We work in silence, desperately trying to get the level far enough down so that we can just pull them out. But when we've got the vicar out, and we're left with Maria's mum, half sticking out of the ground like some sad tulip, all floppy and hopeless, there's a shout outside the back door.

'Shovels!' I scream – and Maria runs for the last shovel leaning against the wall. 'Door!'

Leaving Ursula and the vicar to paw at the sawdust around Maria's mum, Henry and Maria stand on one side of the door, and I stand on the other. We wait for the door to open. 'Derfs,' I yell at Ursula. 'Get your gun out, ready.'

Outside the door, I can hear ponies on the concrete, and thundering voices. Slaps on the back. It sounds like there are loads of them.

Brrrrrrrrrrrrrrrrrrrrrrrrrrrrrrrrrrr.

The door rolls open; nothing happens for a moment. It must seem dark in here.

'Hey! Prisonerus escapus!' shouts the nearest Roman.

He steps forward and –

Thud. Henry catches him on the back of the neck with the shovel handle.

He falls to the ground.

Thud.

'Yow!' yells another of the Romans and runs backwards.
Thud.

There's a soft hiss and a Derf pellet whizzes through the air and hits one of the Romans on the cheek.

'Keep it up!' yells Maria, thwacking another. 'There — that's for you from me!'

Thud.

'Ow!' yowls a Roman, running into the barn, seeing Ursula with the Derf gun and running straight out again.

'Door!' I shout, and we pull it shut, shoving the unconscious Roman back out through the entrance, just as the vicar finally extracts his wife from the sawdust.

We stand, listening.

The Romans are on all sides.

Guarding both doors.

'Phew,' says Henry.

Ursula produces her camera. A horse whinnies on one side and a goat bleats on the other.

'Oh no, Lucy!' says Henry. 'They'll find her — what did the Romans do to goats?' he asks.

'Eat them,' says Ursula. 'Probably stewed.'

Henry's brick colour turns to pale. 'We have to rescue her. We can't stay here and listen to her being — murdered.'

'We can't stay here anyway, there's nothing to eat,' I say,

thinking with sadness of yesterday's Jammie Dodgers and Mrs Mytych.

Maria's dad's shaking his head, as if he's trying to get water out of his ear. 'What's...? I...' He looks confused.

'You all right, Dad?' asks Maria.

'What am I doing here?' he says, looking down at his wife, still unconscious in his arms. 'What in heaven's name is happening?'

'The Romans?' asks Maria.

But the vicar looks confused and pulls sawdust from his wife's hair.

'How are we going to get out of here?' asks Henry, picking up Derf pellets and packing them into his pockets. 'I mean, there must be thirty of them, and only six of us, and one of those is asleep.'

I look around; we've got three shovels, ten Derf guns and a load of telegraph poles. Something comes to mind, something Dad banged on about in the museum when I was little.

Battering rams. Ancient people were always using battering rams to break in – perhaps we could use one to break out?

Chapter 17

Telegraph poles are heavy. Extraordinarily heavy. I suppose when you think about it, they're a whole tree, minus the fluffy bits. If it wasn't for Henry, and Maria's mum, who has finally woken up, and the fact that one of the telegraph poles is shorter than all the others, we wouldn't stand a chance.

We line up on either side of the pole.

'So what's the plan?' asks Maria.

Everyone stares at Ursula, who points at me.

'The plan is…' I think for a moment. 'The plan is: that we burst through this door, and keep running. However, if we spot Lucy, we stop, grab her, and keep running.'

'But how do we get through the rugby soldiers?' asks Maria's dad, who still looks confused, although not half as confused as Maria's mum, who keeps on staring at her hands and saying little prayers.

'We blast 'em!' says Henry, accidentally firing a load of Derf pellets at Ursula.

'Ow!' she says. 'Henry, you're such a...clot!'

'Sorry,' says Henry, looking at the floor.

'Surprise,' I say, remembering something Dad said about the Trojan Horse. 'It's just a question of the "element of surprise".'

Henry manages to hold a Derf gun in one hand, and the pole in the other. I can't – I have to concentrate on carrying the pole and jam my gun in my jeans.

We listen to the world outside the barn. The Romans are losing focus, chatting and singing rugby songs. Now's our moment.

'One...two...three, go!' I whisper.

Bang!

The door flies open, and we run, bowling through the men lolling outside.

'AAAAAAAAAAAGGGGGGGGHHHHH!' screams Maria. Sawdust floats around us like a swarm of flies, and we race out of the barn towards the loose boxes. A single Roman wanders towards us, leading a goat.

'Lucy!' yells Henry.

'Bleeaat!' calls Lucy and Henry veers so that the lone Roman becomes our target.

'Aaaaaaaarghghghgh!' we shout, closing on him.

'Yow!' he yelps, and runs off to the side. Lucy stands temporarily transfixed by the oncoming pole but as we close on her she sidesteps as if to gallop past us into the empty barn.

'Stop!' I scream. 'Drop the pole.'

Henry grabs Lucy and we run, although Maria's mum doesn't know the meaning of run, so Ursula runs and the rest of us drag Maria's mum over the yard towards the car park.

Behind us, the Romans are gaining, and they're becoming more organised. They're grabbing tools from the stables, and once again a fine collection of dustbin lids, and apart from Derf guns, we've got nothing that'll stop them.

I skid to a halt on the far side of a small horse lorry. Everyone follows, Maria's dad holding his chest, looking alarmingly pink; Henry immediately turns and fires Derf pellets at the oncoming Romans.

Ursula pulls out her camera and films around the side of the truck. A hail of well-aimed pitchforks hits the ground beside her. 'There's Mr Dent,' she says, pointing at the image on her screen. 'Look.'

She's right. He's there in the middle. 'Try and reason with him,' I say.

'Mr Dent!' she calls. 'Mr Dent, this is Ursula Ross.'

For a moment the pitchforks slow down.

'Mr Dent, you're our teacher – and we'd like you to stop throwing things at us.'

There's a silence from the Romans.

'Bargainus?' says one of them.

'Bargainus,' says Ursula.

'Promisus?' says the Roman.

'Yesus,' says Ursula.

BBBBRRRRROOOM, BRROOOOOM.

What? I look round for the noise.

It's the horse truck, someone's started the engine.

'Quick, jump in,' yells Maria from the driving seat. 'There's a door, there.'

I open the door into the part that a horse stands in, and we clamber in, shoving Maria's mum into the corner with the most hay.

'Go!' I shout.

The truck judders backwards out of the car park, brooms and shovels thumping on the roof like scary rain. Maria takes the truck in a couple of reverse circuits, throwing us across the inside and pressing me against the tiny window, before finding a forward gear and kangarooing into the road.

I look towards the scattered Romans and the last thing I see of the riding stables is Mr Dent's confused face darkening with fury.

Chapter 18

Maria's not a great driver.

After we leave the riding stables, houses loom on either side of the truck, tree branches seem to throw themselves at the windscreen and strange screeching sounds reverberate through the hollow horsebox as we scrape along parked cars. We go from really fast to really slow and back again, dropping in and out of potholes, until I think I'm going to be sick.

Just as suddenly as she started, Maria stops, throwing us all to the front of the box. As we hoist her mother to her feet the side door opens.

'Right. Is everyone all right?'

'Where did you learn to drive?' asks Henry, picking horse poo from his trousers.

'I didn't,' she says. 'It's a case of common sense.'

Ursula raises an eyebrow, and films Maria's mum who, seeing the open door, suddenly seems to find her legs and staggers into the daylight.

Maria's taken us to the vicarage behind the church. You almost wouldn't know it was there, surrounded by yew trees. It feels quite safe, although we know the Romans were here before, and could be back again. The only advantage, defensively, is that the back of the vicarage is built into a high stone wall that runs around the churchyard. It has no windows on the church side, so it can only be attacked from the front. The disadvantage is huge windows, and nothing to use as a defensive weapon. Not even a catapult.

'Coffee, I must have a coffee,' mutters Maria's mum, reaching the open front door.

'What a good idea,' says the vicar, following his wife inside.

I stare at their backs. Something's catching in the back of my mind. 'Maria, would you say your father's better or worse than he was yesterday?'

Maria picks a piece of sawdust from her hair. 'Madder, you mean?' She wrinkles up her nose. 'Now you mention it, he was almost normal by the time we left the riding stables. Confused, but not ranting. Why?'

'I don't know, I can't work it out. My parents have become progressively weirder – at no point did they improve; but your dad seemed shocked – he seemed surprised, like we'd woken him up – and those Stone Age people –'

'Bronze Age...' interrupts Ursula.

'Whatever – the people in the statue Stonehenge – they seemed to wake up when you shot at them, Henry.'

'It's like they've been drugged,' says Ursula. 'As if something's poisoned them, and it's got worse and worse.'

'Poison?' says Henry. 'That's about the only thing they haven't tried to kill us with. Talking of which – is there anything to eat here, Maria – I'm absolutely starving.'

We put Lucy into the cupboard under the stairs with all the hay we can find from the horsebox and a bucket of water. A minute later and we're sinking our teeth into a tin of stale chocolates that Maria's dad was given for Christmas. They feel like the first proper thing I've eaten for days; much better than cucumber. Briefly I wonder what's happening at home, and then decide that I don't really want to know. If Mum and Dad and the policeman are already entering the afterlife, then Marcus is in charge. But presumably they couldn't do it without a priest – could they?

I look at the clock. Ten minutes since we got here – it'll take the Romans half an hour on horseback; unless they run, in which case it'll take them a quarter of an hour.

'Have you got a hosepipe?' I ask Maria.

'Yeah – round the side. So,' says Maria, green stuff leaking between her teeth from the chocolate in her mouth, 'what are we doing next?'

Ursula stands up and backs into a corner with her camera. We stare at her. 'Keep talking,' she says. 'I'm just recording it – so that when we're found dead by the world outside, they'll know what happened to us.'

'What? Dead and tied to a stake?' asks Henry.

'Or crucified?' asks Maria.

'Exactly,' says Ursula.

I leave them and walk around the house looking for the outside tap. There is a hosepipe, it's ridiculously long, and I connect it up. I think about taking it back in through the house, but that would mean leaving the door open. We'll have to hope that the Romans don't think about using it on us – but then they didn't have hosepipes in the first century AD, so far as I know, so I suppose it shouldn't even occur to them; but then I don't know very much. I wish I'd paid more attention on Dad's visits to the museum.

I go back in and help myself to an orange cream. Yuk.

I have to eat a strawberry fondant to get rid of the taste. I check the cupboards for weapons while my tongue scrapes all the sugary goo from the roof of my mouth. All I can find is board games, hundreds of board games, and cards and knitting.

'Why,' asks Maria, pushing cushions up against the inside of the huge windows that face the drive, 'isn't everyone affected? Why is it just the adults?'

'But it isn't just the adults,' I say. 'My little brother Finn seems to be loving the whole business of mummification.'

'And that's not just because he's four?' asks Maria.

I think about it, also wondering how Maria's parents would feel if I wrenched the door from the cupboard to use as a shield. 'No – he's definitely "infected".'

Ursula's camera swings round on to me. '"Infected"? Like in *Plague of the Living Dead*?'

'Yes, I suppose so.'

'So do you think there's some kind of tiny mosquito flying around, biting them, making them all…' says Ursula.

'Historical?' says Henry, experimenting with a toffee sandwich, in which the bread is also made of toffee. 'An historical mosquito – one that has fed on the blood of mummies?'

'Mummies haven't got blood, stupid,' says Ursula.

'It's definitely got worse,' I say. 'Before the weekend, my

mum was still calling me Sam – now I'm "Revered Second Son". Presumably there'll be a point where she doesn't recognise me any more.'

We've blocked the windows up, but apart from coal and books there's a terrible shortage of ammunition. The actual chairs, I suppose, would fit through the windows.

'Perhaps it's in the water?' says Henry, through the toffee. 'I mean, cholera – or was it typhoid? One of them got into London's drinking water and that's how loads of people died, and lots of diseases in the developing world are waterborne, and Prince Albert died of water that came from Queen Victoria's toilet and –'

'How on earth do you know that?' interrupts Ursula.

Henry turns a light shade of brick. 'Been to Osborne House, on the Isle of Wight. Caravan holiday.'

'Sorry, Henry, it can't be the water,' I say. 'Otherwise we'd all have it – and it can't be the food, because in my house, we all eat the same thing.'

Ursula nods. 'Mine too.'

I sit back on a battered cushionless sofa, aware of Henry's jaw struggling with three layers of toffee, and listening for the Romans.

'I know tha-at my re-de-e-mer liveth!' a high, out-of-key, quavery voice screeches down the stairs.

'Oh yeah – Mum's being a nun – a singing nun. Sorry.' Maria goes over to shut the door.

'It's a government conspiracy,' says Ursula. 'Honestly, this way, we don't notice the lack of services, or government.'

I stick a nut cluster in my mouth, and wish I hadn't. And then I have a thought. 'Ursula?'

'What?'

'Have you got all the film you've taken since that first day when Dad took us to the museum?'

'Yes – I've got the memory cards in here. I wasn't going to leave them in the house, in case the Greeks did actually destroy Troy.'

'Ah.' I have a brief image of the two halves of the corrugated iron horse I saw behind the takeaway. It's probably finished by now. ' Maria, do you by any chance have a computer?' I ask. 'One that would take Ursula's film?'

'Yes – in the cellar, with the games box.'

'It's going to take me a while to edit it properly,' says Ursula. 'We might not have that long.'

'You're so quick at editing, you'll be fine,' I say, trying to make her think it was her idea. 'Anyway, we could just watch it uncut.'

'Yes,' says Ursula as if I was three. 'But I need to take

these bits out.' She points at the display screen on the back of the camera. 'The tiny bits of filming that we did do for *Werewolves*.' She sighs. 'We're never going to get to make that film; all this mayhem's completely destroyed our chances of winning.'

I say nothing. It strikes me that the FLAP film prize is far less important than life and death, but then I'm not going to be the person to point that out.

Maria doesn't tread so carefully. 'You're worried about one of your lousy movies, now?' she says. 'What was this one about?'

'Oh, nothing,' snaps Ursula. Maria rolls her eyes.

'And LO! The barbarian hordes did batter down the doors!' Maria's dad shouts from the kitchen. 'And I, the last man of God, did throw myself upon their spears!'

Maria's brow furrows. 'Blast! I thought he was all right – he's off again.'

Chapter 19

Maria's dad's right – the barbarian hordes are back.

The first sign is a croquet ball flying through the window. As I fill my hands with lumps of coal to fire back, Maria's brother, Amos, appears in the room.

'What the...' he says, staring at the broken glass. 'I've just had a message from Marcus – something's going down at the church.'

'What?' I ask, as another ball crashes through the glass.

Henry's up against the bottom of the window, firing furiously through the broken glass, the Derf gun clattering.

'I don't know, he didn't say – he just said to get down there.'

I lob chunks of coal out onto the drive, but I'm firing blind because of the cushions. 'But we can't even keep the Romans off your parents at the moment.'

'Surrenderus!' comes the cry from outside.

'No way,' shouts Maria. 'Quick, Ursula, this way for the computer – it's quite whizzy, my uncle bought it for me.'

Another ball flies through the glass, and Henry drops the Derf gun in favour of a cricket bat leaning up against the fireside. 'C'mon, Sam, bowl it for me.'

As the contents of the garage fly through the window, Henry faces me, and I gently bowl the croquet ball at him. He whacks it hard and it flies out through the only whole pane of glass.

'Yow!' screams someone outside.

'Yay!' shouts Amos, firing walnuts through a gap in the cushions with an elastic band and the back of a chair.

'Amos – text Marcus and tell him to get as many people as possible and come here,' I say.

Crash.

'And bring weapons, look in my room, bring Derf guns, anything that'll help.'

Another croquet ball whizzes through an empty window frame.

Whack!

Henry returns it with force.

I bowl six large chunks of coal to Henry, who sends them hard towards the Romans.

'He's on his way,' says Amos, shoving his phone in his pocket and searching on the mantelpiece for something to fire. He grabs a handful of wizened conkers and shoots them out one at a time. 'They're coming on bikes.'

I creep up to the side of the window and look out.

The Romans are lined up on ponies. Mr Dent's still looking thunderous, and above me I can hear the vicar yelling at them. It's not helping. Maria's mother's singing to the mirror in the hall, oblivious to the racket outside. They've got a cage, with what looks like a sleeping tabby cat inside.

Lions?

Is that what they were going to kill Maria and her parents with? I suppose you might die of cat breath.

'Tell him the Romans are on the driveway. That there's a hosepipe connected up on the side of the house,' I say, as the Romans wheel out a strange machine made from a metal bucket, a wheelbarrow, bungees and a door. As I watch, Mr Dent empties a load of balls of string into a bucket of black goo. He hooks out one of the balls of string, now black and gloopy, and leans over the bucket. I can't really see what he's doing, but I think he's striking a match.

'Oh no,' I say, watching the little ball of string ignite.

'It might be Greek fire; I'm sure Dad told me about it. They're going to firebomb us.'

The first flaming ball of string flies through the window, and although Henry makes a valiant attempt to strike it back, it just sticks to his cricket bat and goes on burning.

'Aaaaaahhh!' screams Henry, and lobs the whole bat out through the window.

'Eeeek!' squeals a Roman.

Another firebomb lands on the threadbare carpet. 'Now what?' says Amos.

I reach for a vase of wilted roses and pour the water over the little fire but it doesn't make any difference, the water just evaporates.

'Tar,' says Maria, appearing in the doorway. 'Water won't put it out – try this.' She grabs a tapestry from a chair and drops it over the ball of flaming string. It might or might not go out, but we can't see it any more.

'Come down – look at the movie,' says Maria.

'I can't leave,' I say, 'there are too many of them.' A flaming broom crashes onto the floor.

While Henry and I stamp on it, Amos's phone rings. We listen while he listens, the flames creeping around our shoes.

'Yeah – just outside on the right? Really long – I think

122

it'll – yeah – could you spray some in here – we're on fire. Great.'

Before he's even put the phone back in his pocket, a blast of icy-cold water sprays in through the window and a hail of Derf pellets clatters onto the floor. I run to the edge of the window, and peer out. Behind the Romans, Ricky and his sister sneak past the back of the horsebox, followed by Will Katanga and some of Marcus's friends.

'Yyaaaaarghghghghgh!' screams a Roman, caught in the spray, and a horse whinnies in horror. Two of the ponies take off across the vicarage lawn, dumping their riders under the monkey puzzle tree, while a third rears and gallops off out of the drive.

'Yay!' shouts Henry – but Mr Dent isn't running anywhere. Calmly, he ties his horse to the horsebox and grabs a pitchfork. Marcus, who is holding the hosepipe, hands it to Ricky's older sister and picks up a croquet ball. Behind him, Ricky races across the lawn towards the two runaway ponies, leaps onto one, and pulls a length of broken branch from a tree.

The pony, presumably aware that it now has someone who can ride on its back, calmly trots across the grass until it's directly behind Mr Dent. Mr Dent is watching Marcus, who I suspect is wishing that Mr Dent was actually a virtual enemy, while Ricky is watching Mr Dent. Mr Dent raises his pitchfork. I don't know if he means to run, or to throw it – but Ricky's there, right there, crunching the branch into the back of Mr Dent's head at such speed, Mr Dent doesn't even turn.

For a second, nothing happens, and then, like some giant statue, Mr Dent crashes to the ground.

'I think we'll mop up now,' says Amos, lobbing the smoking rug through the window. 'Go on, go and do whatever it is.'

Chapter 20

'Right,' says Ursula. 'Ready? Here we go.'

She presses 'play' and we start with the museum. Ursula likes the hand-held camera style of filming, so the picture wobbles up and down the screen and sometimes you can't see who's talking. We get to see the new shiny display cases, and then the camera zooms in on Dad's hands playing with an Egyptian mask.

'Look – he's already doing it there,' says Henry, jabbing the screen. 'Being Egyptian.'

Feet clatter on the stairs and Amos rushes in, carrying the coal scuttle. 'Ammunition,' he says, filling it from the coal box in the corner before vanishing back up the stairs.

On the screen is our classroom descending into feathery chaos with Miss Primrose. Although the camera keeps trying to focus on the feathers, you can quite clearly see her sipping her coffee and building the temple. The camera pulls in on her eyes. She's looking into the distance, as if she's watching a film inside her head.

'She's completely bonkers by then,' says Henry as the camera pulls in on Miss Primrose, a day or so later, wearing the wetsuit covered in fluff. In her hands is Tiny Tim's growler, groaning like a sheep.

'Look – see,' I say. 'It was her, she did steal his heart.'

She talks about appeasing the gods and I remember the things we saw in the museum. I shiver. I'd said she couldn't do anything without building a temple, but pyramids of one sort or another are popping up all over town, and I suppose she might have a builder friend or something. We really ought to find her and take her out of action, for her own good, and Henry's.

A tiny child's miserable face fills the screen, then the camera pulls back to show Tiny Tim savaged on the tarmac before cutting to a blurry image of traffic cones and feet. The camera must have been lying on its side at this point, because the feet and cones keep passing, and all we can hear is the tinny bird-call music from the staffroom. The camera cuts to the policeman, lolling against the fence. It zooms in on his eyes.

'Mad, definitely mad,' says Henry.

'I should have noticed,' I say. 'He was never going to be any use.'

The film pans out across the field, catching Mr Dent leaning back ready to throw his javelin. Although Ursula was a long way away when she filmed it, both Henry and I flinch as it flies through the air.

'Whew!' says Maria. 'That was a bit close!'

Henry nods. 'He was definitely trying to kill us.'

The film goes dark and juddery, and I realise that this is the Stonehenge night. It's weird to watch. There's me, on the right, pushing the pushchair, and then me pulled by the hair, and then me at the back of the circle. Henry and Lucy cross the sightline and Henry ties her to the pushchair before loading up with Derf guns and his papier mâché sun head. Then there's me, up in the air, five feet off the ground. The camera zooms in on the first Derf bullets hitting home and back onto Henry hiding inside the washing-machine box.

'Stop!' says Maria. 'Play that bit again, where the pellet hits the man with the scarf on his head.'

'*What?*' he says.

'Again,' says Maria.

'*What?*'

'Again,' says Maria.

'*What?*'

'What are we looking at?' asks Henry.

'Oh yes. He's speaking English – not grunt,' I say.

'Just like Dad – look in his eyes. It's as if he's in a trance, and then – the trance goes – as if, for a moment, he's back to normal,' says Maria.

'And what precisely does that tell us?' asks Ursula.

Maria looks at me. 'No idea,' I say, 'but I'm sure it tells us something.'

The next shot is the back of a green wheelie bin stuck with arrows – all you can see is plastic – but there's a load of screaming in the background. The camera wobbles and points at a patch of tarmac, but the screaming goes on. Feet appear, and the camera wobbles again, until we're looking up the skirts of a mass of women. Ursula must have stood up at that point, because the film focuses on the Parish Hall, which is now apparently empty. Henry's back fills the screen.

'*Food*,' he says, pointing at the plate.

The camera stays outside the hall. My back in a green fleece crosses the screen, and there's a bloodcurdling scream.

Ursula yelps, but holds the camera steady – a chair waves from the left of the screen, and the camera moves up until we can see the person holding it.

'That's Mrs Mytych,' says Maria.

'Yes,' says Ursula. 'I don't know what she thought she was.'

There's a close-up shot of Mrs Mytych's face.

'Stop,' I say. 'Look at her eyes – they're different.'

We stare at the computer. Mrs Mytych doesn't look like she's in a trance, she looks like she's terrified.

'Henry, when we went to her shop, do you think she was mad – or scared?'

A croquet ball rattles down the coal hole. Henry tosses it from one hand to the other. 'Well, now you mention it, scared. All that stuff about dressing up – was she trying to warn us?'

'So it isn't just that all the adults turn funny at eighteen, like in a post-apocalyptic fantasy young adult thing,' says Ursula.

'Nor that it's in the water, or the air, otherwise we'd have it, and so would Mrs Mytych,' says Henry.

'And it hasn't come through mobile phones, or Amos would be mad,' says Maria.

'It must be a plot,' says Ursula, watching her parents fortifying the house. 'Some evil genius has taken over their minds for some dastardly purpose. But how?'

'Could be a plot, I suppose,' says Henry. 'Like in *Day of*

the Zombie Aliens when they're actually being manipulated by the vampire toad that lives in the tube station?'

Ursula stares at him. 'Very like,' she says, as if noticing Henry for the first time.

There's a shot of me riding Henry's bike across the town square, dodging bonfires and then screeching to a halt outside the museum. The film flickers over the museum cafe, resting on the window. Through the reflection of Henry, we can see through the glass. There are the bags of coffee and chocolate, and the giant cakes, Stonehenge and the Acropolis, but they've taken a hammering, with chunks missing.

'Wow!' says Maria. 'They look good.'

'Don't they, and those people look as if they're enjoying them,' says Henry, pointing to the top corner of the screen.

He's right. At the time, we only saw the scary woman standing guard, but the camera shows six people dancing around the table in the middle of the cafe, drinking chocolate from a fondue set, spooning cup after cup down their throats.

Something occurs to me. 'Have all your parents been to the museum cafe?' I ask.

Henry and Ursula nod, but Maria shakes her head. 'It's too expensive, my mum and dad wouldn't go there.

Anyway, they have to go to so many coffee mornings I can't believe it would be a treat.'

'So you really don't think they've ever been – never even bought anything from it?'

Maria shakes her head. 'Never, definitely never.'

'Hmmm,' says Henry. 'Pity – good theory though, Sam.'

We watch the rest of the film in silence. I'm disappointed; I really wanted it to be the cafe – it would explain everything.

More images flash past on the screen. Henry's mother wearing a lampshade, Lucy, the riding stables, Mr Dent's look of fury, the journey in the horsebox. All of it plays back while I try to remember Mum's habits; what does she do all day? I realise that I don't really know. Go swimming? Eat stuff? Go to cafes?

When the film finishes, we sit in silence listening to the battle dying overhead.

Maria closes down the computer. 'Right,' she says, 'now what?'

'Come on!' shouts Marcus, from the top of the cellar steps. 'You lot! We've got things to do and people to save!'

Chapter 21

'But we need to understand why it's happening,' I say.

'No time for that. Complete meltdown at the church.'

'What have you done with the Romans?' asks Henry.

'Horsebox; we tied them up with haynets and shut them in.'

I try not to imagine it, but I can't shake the idea of Mr Dent wrapped in a haynet.

We follow Marcus through the house; he's whooping and yelping like a two-year-old – I haven't seen him move so much in years.

'Yay!' says Amos, doing a high five with Marcus. 'We did it!' He's carrying a bag of coal around his neck, like a refugee expecting to get very cold. 'We've beaten them.'

'Av-e Ma-ri-i-a. Aaaaaaaaaa-ve…'

'What's that noise?' asks Marcus, freezing in the doorway.

'Mum,' says Maria, opening the hall door, and closing it again, as her mother draws breath. 'Sorry, she's...she's...'

'Mad again?' Henry suggests. 'How's she managed to get mad since we came back?'

'That, Henry,' I say, collecting Derf pellets and jamming them in my pocket, 'is a very good point. How has she managed to get mad here, in the house?'

'You don't want to use those,' says Marcus, pointing at the Derf pellets. He holds out a handful of hazelnuts. 'Found them in the larder, eight years past their sell-by date; they fit in the Derf gun barrel, and they sting.'

I look at the little nuts. They must *really* hurt. I think about Mr Dent and the pitchfork. Just as well, really.

We pick our way through the broken glass, and out through the kitchen door. Ricky's pulled all the ponies together, and tied them to the outside of the horsebox, while his sister picks up croquet balls from all over the garden. Six of Marcus's friends lie on the grass, reloading Derf guns with hazelnuts.

Whirrrrrrrr. Ursula's filming again. 'S'funny,' she says, 'it's getting awfully dark considering it's only lunchtime.'

'Altogether, I reckon there are nineteen of us,' says Marcus, leading the way down the vicarage garden to a gate in the wall to the churchyard. 'If we leave Ricky looking after the ponies, and guarding the Roman legion, then we'll be OK.'

'Great,' I say, wondering at what point Marcus was elected leader. 'But we really need to find the root of the problem. I mean, Maria's parents have managed to get bonkers again, even after they'd sobered up.' I duck under a low branch. 'Until we find out what's causing it, wrapping people in haynets isn't going to help for long –' A thought strikes me. 'Maria, where do your parents get their coffee? Your mum did say "coffee" when we came back from the stables.'

We brush through the yew trees; they're so dense and dark, I can only just make out the weird sounds coming from the church, the loudest of which is the bell.

'It sounds like cats,' says Maria. 'Yes – she did say coffee – they drink gallons of the stuff. The supermarket, I suppose, although –'

'Yoooooooowwwwwwwlllllll!'

'Heeeeellllllppppppppp!'

'What is it?' asks Maria.

Marcus stops and points.

On the church roof – the very high church roof – are a load of tiny children, and standing over them, balanced on the window of the tower, is a strange figure dressed

135

as what appears to be a giant pipe-cleaner. Inside the tower, someone's banging the bell, and a cacophony of tweets and whistles rings out across the church yard.

'That's Miss Primrose, and she must have someone with her making that noise,' mutters Henry. 'What on earth is she doing?'

And suddenly my dream comes back, mixed with the horrible image of Tiny Tim's missing heart.

'I got it completely wrong; she doesn't want to kill *you*, Henry – she wants as many hearts as possible to bring back the real sun,' I say. 'This darkness, it's the eclipse.'

Chapter 22

There are adults clustered around the church, but they aren't doing anything useful. A couple of Egyptians are worshipping a tombstone, and someone's having a Victorian picnic by a vaulted grave.

Two men standing in the tower, wearing not much more than cardboard headdresses, blow into scraps of bamboo and bang on an oil drum. I'm guessing this is ceremonial Aztec unmusic.

I look along the roof. There's honestly nothing stopping the children falling, except some guttering and their fingernails.

'How did they get up there?' asks Henry.

'There's a staircase in the tower, and a door – they use it for maintenance,' says Maria.

Ursula points her camera at the roof and starts filming.

'They're mostly year ones,' she says. 'How did she get hold of them?'

'I suppose their mums and dads took them to school,' says Maria.

'Or forgot to pick them up,' I say, staring up at the roof and trying to think of a way to get them down.

The sky loses a little more light. It's weird, like someone's pulled a grey curtain over the day. Birds cluster in the tall yews, and fall silent.

The only bird sounds now come from the tower.

'Do you know how long the eclipse was supposed to last?' I ask Henry.

He shrugs. 'Nope, but it's not a proper one, only a half-one.'

I look up. Miss Primrose is gazing at the sky, clutching a huge curved knife that might or might not be cardboard. The little kids are gazing at her, transfixed and in most cases crying.

'Are they on both sides of the roof?' I whisper to Maria.

She slips off around the church to check and comes back with the good news that they're all on our side.

'Mattresses,' I say. 'I think the best bet would be loads of mattresses. Have you any at the vicarage?'

'There's all the camping gear, for the scouts.'

'I'll come with you,' I say, handing my Derf gun to Henry. We run back through the bushes in the odd half-light.

'Maria, what did you say about your parents and the coffee?'

'Oh yeah – they always buy it from the supermarket.' We crash through the front door and Maria charges down the cellar steps and wrenches open a cupboard door. 'Here.' A pile of foam rubber mats falls out on the floor.

'Always from the supermarket?' We grab armfuls of the mats and struggle back up the stairs.

'Almost always. But,' she says, 'my uncle, the same one that gave me the computer, brought them a packet the other day, expensive beans; it's in the kitchen.'

'I'll be with you in a sec.' I dump the mats in the hall and dodge past Maria's mum, who's serenading herself in the hall mirror. There on the kitchen top is a large white paper bag, MUSEUM CAFE, ONE KILO, Ground Colombian Roast printed across it. I pull open the top. At least half has gone. A cafetière stands on the counter top, mostly drunk. I put my hands against it and it's warm. So they've had at least two cups each since we came back.

'YES!' I say to the vicarage cat. 'YES!' He looks up at me as if I was an alien, and slips out through the cat flap.

I take the bag of coffee and empty it over the flower beds outside.

'YES!'

I sniff the empty bag. There's nothing odd about it, it just smells of coffee. I open the cupboards and check for other things. There's a bar of museum chocolate, also half eaten. I sniff it, tempted to take a bite, and bung it in the bin.

And then I have another thought. Chocolate? Wasn't that ice cream that Mum gave me home-made? It tasted great, but perhaps that's why I had that strange dream? And Finn, he's been stuffing the chocolate down – every time I've seen him recently he's had chocolate around his face. That'll be why he mummified the cat.

'YES!'

I run back into the hall, fill my arms with the mattresses and head towards the church, meeting Henry and three of Marcus's friends coming back with Maria for more padding.

'I've solved it,' I shout. 'It's coffee and chocolate!'

'What?' says Henry, running along beside me.

I reach the church and dump the mattresses next to Maria's.

'From the cafe. You don't necessarily have to eat it there,

but bringing it home is just as bad. Maria's parents had a huge bag of coffee – and some chocolate.'

'C'mon,' says Marcus. 'Stop faffing around with those things; let's get up there and take out the guys in the tower.'

'No, let's wait,' I say. 'Otherwise the tinies'll fall off and there'll be nothing to break their fall.'

'So? It's collateral damage,' says Marcus, looking as mad as Maria's dad.

'Marcus! This is real – wake up. Those are real children up there crying.'

Marcus swallows, clicks the chamber on his Derf gun and nods. 'Fair enough – so what are we going to do?'

'We're going to coax her down.'

'How?'

I look behind to see Henry and Maria dragging a double mattress over the gravestones.

'Henry? Do you think you could be the sun at last?'

Chapter 23

In the vicarage garage, we find a piece of plywood from the nativity, and a blunt saw.

'But I thought she didn't need me. I thought she was happy killing the little ones,' says Henry, swinging the vicar's prize cricket bat.

'Oh she is – quite happy; she thinks their hearts will bring back the sun – but she's not counting on the sun god turning up. Try to cut out a couple of circles, about the size of tea trays,' I say. 'I'll look and see what else there is.'

The vicarage garage is fantastic. It's like every play that ever went on in the church hall has finally died in here. There are bags of hats, swords, wings, pieces of furniture, giant cauldrons, golden geese, anything and everything. I search the hat bag, pull out a handful of ostrich feathers and plunge through all the bric-a-brac looking for anything appropriate.

On the piano, I find a box of multicoloured feather boas; behind it, a stuffed parrot nailed to a hat stand. Grabbing both, I fight my way past coat racks and parasols to the doorway, passing a huge length of rope which I stick inside my backpack, just in case.

Something that looks like an old-fashioned record player horn sticks out from under a broken leather chair. I don't know whether I need it but it looks interesting. It turns out to be a megaphone, with a battery and button.

'Yay!' I shout. 'How are you getting on?'

'I'm nearly done,' pants Henry. 'Hard work, this saw.'

'Here, take this,' I say, throwing Henry the tinfoil from Mrs Mytych. 'Wrap it all the way round both sides.' I find a Roman-style brown tunic, a pile of paper masks and a long multicoloured sash on a clothes rail and run back to the doorway.

'Right, time to dress you, Henry.'

With the tunic, a band of upholstery cord and the ostrich feathers, he just looks stupid. But when I tie the parrot around his waist with the sash, and poke the boas inside his collar so that they hang down, he starts to look weird. I wrap an army helmet in tinfoil and jam it on his head with the last of the ostrich feathers poking out of the top.

'The sun?' says Henry doubtfully. 'This isn't anything like the sun costume I was making for Ursula's film.'

'Well, this looks at least a little like the costumes they illustrated in the museum,' I say, taping the silver discs to the back of his wrists with duct tape. 'They've got this god – Huitza-something. He was the one that sprang out and killed his sister and his four hundred brothers. Have you seen a torch anywhere?' Henry points at a large red torch standing by the door. 'Thanks. There was a picture of Huitza-whatsit in the museum. He was a big cheese. And I think, according to the way she's dressed in that wetsuit, that Miss Primrose thinks she's a priest, dressed as Quetzalcoatl, in which case, she's probably sacrificing the children to you.'

I take one of the paper masks and cover it thickly with tinfoil. The elastic just fits over the helmet and the feathers and the mask pings onto his face.

Henry nods; the parrot nods with him. Now it's out of the garage, I can see how moth-eaten it is.

'Can you walk?' I ask.

He nods.

'And talk?'

He shakes his head, and tries to speak. 'Iths a bith closthe in th'here,' he mumbles.

'OK,' I say, picking up the megaphone, 'I'll talk, you just look godly.'

'What'th we goin' the doo?'

'What are we going to do? We're going to fool her. You're going to wave your arms, and I'm going to speak, and we're going to hope that Maria gets back with enough mattresses in time.'

We struggle back to the church. Henry can't see very well, so he blunders into the trees, and sheds feathers and scraps of tinfoil, but hopefully from Miss Primrose's point of view on the roof it won't matter. About a hundred metres from the tower is a gardener's store. I pull out a stepladder and with difficulty Henry clambers onto the churchyard wall. It allows me to stand in a thick yew tree just underneath, with the megaphone and the torch.

Maria passes us, dragging a pile of camping mats, and two of Marcus's friends follow with another double mattress. 'We're getting there,' she says. 'Rani's turned up with a wheelbarrow of cushions – her little brother's up there, and Will and his sister have brought their trampoline, but it's not very big. And what you say about the coffee – I've spread the word.'

'Brilliant, Maria. Ready?' I call up to Henry.

'Umph,' he mumbles.

'I have to take that as a yes, Henry; here we go.'

'OH PRIEST OF MINE,' my voice booms across the churchyard. All the crows roosting in the yew trees take off and shriek before landing again. 'I AM HONOURED BY YOUR OFFERING.'

The crows take off and land again, and I listen, in case Miss Primrose answers.

The drumming stops.

'Anything happen?' I ask, shining the torch onto Henry's tinfoil circles so that they glitter in the half-darkness. I have to say, he looks really impressive. He moves his arms slowly and in what I imagine is a godlike way.

'A tedthy's fafllen off t'the woof,' says Henry, above me.

'OH PRIEST OF MINE,' I say. 'THESE CHILDREN THAT YOU OFFER, THEY ARE TOO SMALL. THEY NEED TO GROW INTO BIGGER CHILDREN.' I look up at the still dark sky. 'I WILL ONLY COME BACK IF YOU CAN GIVE ME BIG CHILDREN. TAKE THESE SMALL CHILDREN FROM THE TEMPLE, AND GIVE ME THE HEARTS OF TEENAGERS.' I peek out through the bushes, to see if Marcus and his mates are still there.

They are, although at least one of them's backing off.

Silence. No drumming, no bird whistles.

'Anything?' I call up to Henry.

'The's thinkin',' he says.

'Oh great Lord.' It's Miss Primrose's voice. 'Give me time to take these children down; I will bring back the larger children, just as soon as I can. Don't disappear from the earth quite yet.'

There's squealing and crying from the kids on the roof. 'Is she moving them?' I call up to Henry.

'Yeth, annuver tedith's faafllen off vough,' he says.

'I GIVE YOU FIVE OF YOUR MINUTES TO RETURN THEM SAFELY TO THE GROUND, OR I WILL TAKE THE YEAR OFF AND YOU CAN LIVE IN DARKNESS.'

'Gooth one!' says Henry, waving his arms majestically.

'Stay there,' I say, running for the tower, still with the megaphone in my hand. 'Marcus,' I shout.

'Yeah – little bro – was that you?' He gives me a high five.

'Yes – but can you grab her the moment she comes down?'

Amos nods. 'Yeah – call it done,' he says, clicking the Derf gun. 'We've called for reinforcements.' As he says it, two of Marcus's friends flatten one of the drummers and pin his arms behind his back.

We wait, and the first of the little kids runs out of the church, tear-stained and panicky. Maria scoops them up and cuddles them. Ursula just films them. 'I gather it's the coffee?' she says from behind the camera.

'Yes – I worked it out. Mrs Mytych is OK because she only drinks stuff from her shop. Everyone else must have bought coffee or chocolate in the cafe, or from the museum shop, and is drinking it at home – or at the rugby club or the Women's Union.'

'I thought as much,' says Ursula. 'I wondered how long it would take for you to work it out.'

I can't be bothered to argue with her, and sink onto the nearest gravestone. I suddenly feel desperately tired and hungry. I'd no idea history was so bloodthirsty or violent. It's exhausting; how did anyone survive?

'Gnananananananahhhhhh.' I turn, just in time to see Mr Dent launching a pitchfork at Marcus.

'Marcus!' I yell, but luckily Mr Dent's aim is off and he hits a headstone instead.

Marcus turns and fires at Mr Dent, Amos too, and behind them I see Miss Primrose leaving the church, with a look of determination on her face.

'Henry!' I shout, pointing.

Behind me, there's a crash, as Henry presumably doesn't

quite make it down the ladder. From the lychgate, half a dozen games box players emerge blinking into the half-light, and fire at Mr Dent and his fellow Romans. I duck between them, following Miss Primrose through the side gate and along the street. Henry joins me, shedding feathers and tinfoil down the road.

'Wath are we thoing to tho?' he asks.

'Stop her,' I answer, 'so she can't damage anyone.'

Chapter 24

Miss Primrose walks fast. She's not put off by the battles we pass, nor does she seem to be trying to catch older children to sacrifice.

'When are we thoing to thrab her?' asks Henry.

'Now? Soon,' I say, breaking into a jog.

We swing into the main square. The museum stands locked before us, while smoke pours out of the cafe next door.

Miss Primrose stops.

'Now!' I say, and we leap forward, grabbing her. One arm each.

'Wha—?!' she yelps, then, seeing Henry, drops to her knees.

'Mith Primrothe,' he says. 'I —'

'Shh,' I say, pointing at my mouth.

As the last shred of tinfoil floats from the sun discs on

his wrists, I realise I'd never planned on Miss Primrose meeting Henry close up.

I rush behind him. 'OH SERVANT,' I bellow. 'YOU SEEK SOMETHING?'

'Oh master of the sun, I seek the elixir.'

'Elithier?' says Henry.

'The precious liquid by which I become close to you and Your Majesty.'

'WHAT ELIXIR IS THIS?' I ask.

'I know not whence it comes,' says Miss Primrose.

'DOES IT COME FROM YONDER SHOP?' I say.

'Henry Waters?' says Miss Primrose. 'Is that you?'

'Yeth,' says Henry, tightening his grip on her arm.

I look round Henry, to Miss Primrose. Her eyes have changed. They look almost normal.

She stares at her arm, at the feathered wetsuit.

'What's the...?'

I rush round and grab her other arm.

'Miss Primrose, I'm sorry about this,' I say, pulling the length of rope out of my backpack.

'Buth ith's for your own gooth,' says Henry.

And we tie her firmly to what's left of the museum bus stop.

*   *   *

152

Henry and I stand outside the cafe. Inside, it's almost completely dark, but we can see that the chocolate fondue dance is still going, although some people are now sparked out on the floor.

'How arth thwe goin' tho do this?' he asks.

I look at him; he's tatty, but he's still dressed like a god – well, sort of. 'Henry, I think you're going to have to act. Be godly, think godly. Persuade them that you're a god, and that way we should be able to get into the kitchen, which is, I think, the source of the problem.'

He pulls himself up, and I straighten his feathers and his tin helmet, and tuck the dead parrot back into his belt. 'Ready?' I ask.

He nods. We walk up the steps and stop in front of the chocolate fondue party. Mr Crump, the builder, stops thwacking the table with a hammer and stares. Two of the women freeze and a third drops to her knees. I look past them to the kitchen; I'm pretty sure that's where we need to be.

Henry stands and looks godly, then kicks me. 'OH MINIONS!' I bellow. 'I COME ONLY TO WATCH YOUR ANTICS. ALLOW ME TO ENTER THE INNER SANCTUM.'

Miraculously, the fondue dancers step aside, and Henry floats forward, exuding godliness, tiptoeing through the lake of chocolate pumping across the floor. I keep as close to him as I can. I don't want them to realise I'm not a god.

Just as we're about to get into the kitchen at last, something from outside makes me turn around.

'Hey!' It's Ursula and Marcus, and some way behind, a limping Mr Dent, leaning on his pitchfork, his face red with fury.

I hesitate in the kitchen door. I can't think how to get Ursula in but leave Mr Dent outside, but Henry turns around to address the fondue dancers. 'THE THE TWO ARE MY FAITHFUL FOLLOTHWERS.' He points at Ursula and Marcus. 'BUTH HE,' he points at Mr Dent, 'THE HROWMAN, IS AN ENEMY.'

Well done Henry.

The dancers part to let Marcus and Ursula through, but surge forward, slippery with chocolate and armed with sponge and cream, to stop Mr Dent and his pitchfork.

'IN!' I shout, shoving Henry through the kitchen door and dragging Ursula and Marcus behind as squares of cake whistle through the air.

We rush to shut the door, squashing a piece of fruit sponge in the frame. Henry grabs a chair and wedges it under the door handle. 'Phew!' he says, peeling off his mask. 'That was close.'

'And?' says Ursula, running the camera over the counter tops, filming every slice of cake and every pie.

'It's here, it's got to be here,' I say.

'What are we looking for?' asks Marcus.

'Something that means that the coffee and probably the chocolate that the cafe sells is in some way contaminated.'

'Like this?' asks Marcus, clambering up onto the counter top and pointing at a large grille that sits over the coffee roasting machine.

'What is it?' asks Henry.

'Dunno,' says Marcus, holding his hand up to the grille. 'But it's letting in cold air from outside.'

I climb up next to him and between us, we pull the metal grille out of the slot on the wall. It isn't just a grille but a whole air conditioning unit. It comes out easily and Marcus yanks the plug out of the wall.

'I can't see through, though,' says Marcus. 'It's just too high, but I can see electric light on the other side.'

'Henry,' I say. 'Could you?'

Ursula strips Henry of his parrot and his boas and we haul him up onto the counter top. Using a sack of flour for extra height, he thrusts his head through the hole in the wall.

'Ha,' he says, laughing.

'What? Henry? Do get on with it,' says Ursula.

The rest of us are more polite.

'It's the museum – the room with all the dust and the mummy: the museum restoration room.' Henry stands on the counter top, his face dripping with sweat. 'If that was an air conditioning unit, then it was sucking in the air on the museum side, and pumping it out on the cafe side. Not just the air, but all the little bits in the air.'

'You mean all the ancient bits of bread and bones and weird unidentified things are ending up in the cafe food?' says Ursula.

'Yes,' says Henry, beaming. 'That's exactly what I mean.'

'You mean there's no evil genius brainwashing our parents? Or a plot by aliens to take over the most boring town in Britain?'

Henry shakes his head. 'No – just an air conditioning unit.'

'Are you sure?' says Marcus.

'He's absolutely sure,' says Ursula. 'Aren't you, Henry?'

Chapter 25

It takes Marcus and his friends the rest of the day to round up the really mad people – that includes Mr Dent, the rest of the Romans and the fondue dancers – and, with some considerable difficulty, lock them in the library. All evening, books fly out through the windows and the rugby songs get louder and less comprehensible.

By midnight, all we can hear is snoring.

'Can we ring someone now?' asks Henry, shreds of feathers still sticking to him.

'Who?' asks Ursula.

'Like the army?' says Henry.

In the end, we settle for ChildHelp, who in turn ring Social Services, who ring NHS Direct, who ring the Department of Education, who ring the Government, who send a bunch of men in white suits with no sense of humour from an airbase in Lincolnshire.

They arrive in helicopters, on ropes, smashing into the Trojan Horse until it just looks like a flattened shed.

They talk to us all night, asking hundreds of questions – and take blood samples from the warring tribes in the library. Then they decide to take blood samples from us, too.

Henry goes forward to offer his arm first; I follow, and Marcus after me.

'No way!' says Ursula. But Henry uses goat techniques on her until she thinks it was her idea.

They sit us in a white plastic tent on the town square, watching reruns of Dr Who.

Eventually the men cordon off the cafe and the museum, and take out all the pieces of the brand-new air conditioning units in huge plastic bags. They take away all the unidentified little boxes for 'examination and testing'. Then they suggest that we children take the rest of the week off school and hand out hundreds of packets of cornflakes and UHT milk.

'Perhaps it's time to go home,' says Ursula, snapping shut the camera case as the men in white suits disappear back inside the museum and the sun rises over the chocolate-covered steps of the museum cafe.

*　*　*

Mum and Dad and the policeman are sitting on plastic chairs in the garden, staring at the pyramid.

'How on earth?' says Dad.

'Goodness,' says Mum, rubbing her head. 'I could kill for a coffee.'

'No you couldn't,' says Marcus, sprinkling the end of a bag of coffee on the last remaining rose bush. 'Not until we've bought new supplies from Mrs Mytych.'

'Perhaps you should take these back,' I say, pointing at the chair and flail that Dad took from the museum.

'Oh no!' he says. 'That's dreadful; how did they get there?'

So, on the way, in the car, I explain.

We pass a digger extracting Queen Victoria from the cricket pitch, and a family driving sheep along the street.

'But how?' says Dad.

'The cafe – there was something wrong with the ventilation system. It joined the museum, so people were eating and drinking little bits of history.'

'Sam, I'm so sorry, it must have been terrifying,' says Dad, driving round the mud huts built on the roundabout.

I think about it. 'It was, a little, but it was also quite funny. Can't you remember anything?'

Dad sits quietly at the traffic lights, thinking.

'I remember having fun, dressing up, making things. It was like being a little kid – just having fun.'

'Hmm,' I say, having an idea.

In August, we had our first town pageant. We argued about the theme. Henry said we should just make it Egyptian, Ursula said that the Renaissance would be best, but in the end we decided that the people of the town should vote on it.

I had fun in the museum with Dad, making a list of all the different cultures and places that people might choose from, and he introduced me to some we hadn't even run into. Ever heard of the Minoans? They lived on Crete and had a bull called the Minotaur. Or the Assyrians? Or even the bog people who buried their dead in bogs. This time, when he took me round it was really interesting, although there were things about the Aztecs that I still felt should remain a mystery.

Henry, Ursula and I put the list together and stuck it through everyone's front door in the entire town. As we went round, we found that not all the houses had gone back to the boring normal way they were before. There were still strange structures strapped onto the front of some houses, and not all the washing hanging out on the lines was twenty-first century.

In the end, the town voted to be Roman on their first pageant. It took no time for Henry's dad and Mr Crump to turn the common into a Roman city, with a temple and a forum and market stalls. Mum made more weird sweets from an original Roman recipe, and she and Finn sold them in aid of the Amateur Dramatic Society, while Ursula's mum made strange pigments out of earth and plants and did terrible brown portraits of everyone. Miss Primrose turned up looking like a Disney Princess, all pink and fluffy and back to normal.

'Ursula, Sam,' she smiled. 'What a lovely idea; what fun to dress up, I love dressing up.'

'We know,' muttered Ursula.

'And Henry,' said Miss Primrose. 'You look...'

Red? Huge? Extraordinary? Like someone wearing a sheet?

'Majestic,' said Miss Primrose. 'Like a god.' She smiled, and a million baskets of kittens jumped into the air.

Henry flushed deep brick and dived into the changing tent. 'What do you think Mr Dent will come as?' he asked, pulling his toga tight around his chest.

'A gladiator,' said Marcus, sharpening his spear. 'But I'll be ready for him.'

'Well, I hope everyone will be well behaved for the

FLAP prize presentation,' said Ursula, who had refused to dress up. 'David Pringle from Hollywood's coming to present it.'

'Don't get your hopes up,' I said.

But I was completely wrong, because David Pringle thought that Ursula's film, made in the end from all the filming she'd done during the historical meltdown, and known as *Egyptian Bread*, was brilliant – a 'post urban comic dystopian apocalyptic fantasy,' he called it, 'informed by historical accuracy and fantastical imagery.' That was fine by us because he gave her a thousand pounds in prize money, which much to my surprise Ursula split three ways – keeping the spare pound for herself, of course.

Reeling from the prizegiving, we moved on to the actual pageant – which was a triumph. Everyone except for Ursula dressed up, and had loads of fun without hurting each other, and even Mrs Mytych came out and joined in as a centurion. Tourists came to stare, and the Mayor declared the Gladiatorial Games open, allowing Mr Dent and Marcus to lay into each other with polystyrene spears and cardboard swords.

They both really enjoyed it.

Epilogue

I'm lying on my bed now, thinking about what to do with my £333. My bed's lovely; I've got my old duvet, my old comfy mattress and my pillows back. The carpet's gone, because of the goat wee, but Mum found one just the same to replace it. Dad's put up a bookshelf over my head; it's wonky but I don't mind. I've got a load of really good history books on it; they're funny and full of facts. I've read them all twice. Dad wants me to do Latin, but that would be going too far.

I've got Henry and Ursula sitting on the floor, reading my old comics. No Lucy though – she's safely back in Henry's garden.

'What are you going to spend it on?' I ask.

'The £333?' Henry says. 'Could go to the Caribbean to watch the cricket, but…'

'Could buy us a new TV, but...' I say.

'We could invest it – in films,' says Henry.

'Really?' says Ursula, her mouth hanging open. 'You'd do that?'

'Yeah,' says Henry. 'We could buy a decent camera. Call ourselves Twenty-first Century Cow,' he says, laughing.

'We could make some really good movies. No zombies, vampires or werewolves. I think they've had their day, don't you?' I ask.

'Would you act in it?' asks Ursula, quietly.

'Yeah,' says Henry. 'So long as you're the director.'

Ursula nods. For once, she can't think of anything to say.

About me and history
F. R. Hitchcock

Dressing up was a big part of my childhood.

I still have the plastic helmet and tabard that marked me out as a Knight of the Round Table, and the cowgirl outfit that Dad brought back from America when I was five, but dressing-up got serious when I first entered the Annual Winchester Guildhall Fancy Dress Competition.

The competition was taken very seriously, by me or Dad I can't remember, but I do remember the thrill of discovering that spray paint cut lovely but toxic swirls in polystyrene, and the discomfort of wearing a genuine WWII German helmet. In all the years I entered, I only won once, and I only won a box of jelly sweets, but I treasured those jelly sweets. They were my just reward for hours of standing very still in uncomfortable costumes.

When I was eight, my tiny school held a pageant in the garden. Hannibal's elephants (the fifth years) broke through the Alps (first years) and jumped on the Romans (third years). Two of us were chosen to represent Carthage. We stood under an apple tree waiting to be battered and defeated by the resurrected Romans – which we did spectacularly, moaning and groaning and throwing ourselves on our plastic swords, while chewing fake blood capsules. It was probably the best fun I ever had at school.

History was a big part of growing up for me. It went along with riding bikes and swinging in trees. Not only did we dress as Saxons, we hung out wherever we might catch a whiff of history and the stories that went with it. Winchester Cathedral was especially rich, with its chests of kingly bones and stories of hearts buried in walls, alongside Victorian diving helmets and tattered campaign flags. With my friends I dredged the river for King Alfred's lost crown, paced huge fields in search of mosaics and ancient animal teeth, and sat on walls watching archaeologists scrape away at the chalk surrounding ancient skulls.

When I learned to drive, I accompanied Dad all over what he called Wessex, and he introduced me to wonderful things and atmospheric places in distant churches, museums and battlefields. Some of them, like the Alfred Jewel in the Ashmolean Museum in Oxford, were significant, many were not – they were just interesting, personal, they belonged to people: a spoon that a Roman lost near Cirencester, a nit comb that survived the shipwreck of the Mary Rose, and a leather boot, said to have been lost by Charles II.

I have continued to absorb the stories in museums. For this book, I visited the British Museum and used the stone tableaux there to decide whether the Aztecs or the Incas were a better source of drama. I chose the Aztecs because they were definitely bloodier, more incomprehensible, and almost certainly more terrifying.

A few years ago I visited the National Museum of Ireland and saw the boat from the Broighter Gold hoard. It is probably the most fragile and beautiful thing I have ever seen. If you have the chance, go and see it; if not, you can find good pictures online.

But although it's not remotely precious, and by no means beautiful, one of my all-time favourite historical objects is the lump of Egyptian bread in the Cairo museum.

That, to me, is real history.

F. R. Hitchcock's Story Adventure

For my next book, uniquely, Hot Key Books have given me (Fleur Hitchcock) the opportunity to canvas YOU for your ideas, allowing me free rein to incorporate as many of those ideas as possible into the book. That book is the sequel to SHRUNK! – the remarkable story of an ordinary boy, Tom Perks, who develops an alarming power, shrinking things. He shrinks a few important things (like the planet Jupiter), and a few unimportant things (the school bully).

Written online weekly, chapter by chapter, from contributions by children all over the country, this book is growing upwards and outwards, filled with wild and exciting ideas, and will be available in a bookshop near you – SOON.

Don't miss SHRUNK!

And look out for the sequel – coming soon!

www.hotkeybooks.com